My Canary Yellow Star

Tundra Books

Copyright © 2001 by Eva Wiseman

Published in Canada by Tundra Books,
481 University Avenue, Toronto, Ontario M5G 2E9

Published in the United States by
Tundra Books of Northern New York,
P.O. Box 1030, Plattsburgh, New York 12901

First U.S. Edition 2002

Library of Congress Control Number: 2001086828

National Library of Canada Cataloguing in Publication Data

Wiseman, Eva, [date]
  My canary yellow star

ISBN 0-88776-533-5

I. Title.

PS8595.I14M9 2001   jC813'.54   C2001-930266-5
PZ7.W57My 2001

We acknowledge the support of the Canada Council for the Arts and
the Ontario Arts Council for our publishing program.

We acknowledge the financial support of the Government of Canada
through the Book Publishing Industry Development Program for our
publishing activities.

Printed and bound in Canada

1 2 3 4 5 6   06 05 04 03 02 01

For my parents

ACKNOWLEDGMENTS

I want to thank my husband and my family for their encouragement, support, and belief in me. I would also like to acknowledge the assistance of the Manitoba Arts Council. The advice of Rabbi Yaacov Benamou about religious issues and James Manishen about music in the 1940s was invaluable. I would also like to thank my editor, Kathy Lowinger, for inspiring me to do my best, and Janice Weaver for her copy-edit.

I feel fortunate to have met the people who shared their stories with me. My special gratitude goes to Judith and Erwin Weiszmann of Winnipeg, Canada. The other people I would like to thank are Alfred Dukes and Frank Weinfeld in Winnipeg; Zsuzsi Weissberger in Montreal; Erica Leon in Los Angeles; and György Vámos, Benedek István Gábor, Márta Hegyi, Károly Landor, Zsuzsa Dobos, István Hollai, and Marietta Weissberger in Budapest, Hungary.

To destroy one life is as if you have destroyed the world.
— The Talmud

CONTENTS

The Occupation

The room was silent except for the scratching of Professor Feldman's chalk. We tried to ignore the sunbeams dancing on our desktops – our new teacher did not take kindly to signs of inattention from his students. Until recently, he had lectured in mathematics at the university, and he had high expectations of us. We were lucky to be taught by such a distinguished scholar – at least that was what my parents told me whenever I complained about him. My friend Judit groaned beside me and we exchanged sympathetic glances before we dove into Professor Feldman's exasperating world of equations.

I had lost track of time grappling with angles and line segments, and the sudden noise of distant thunder startled me. It rolled louder and louder. We raised our eyes to the window. There was no sign of a cloud, yet the thunder outside intensified. Even Professor Feldman seemed puzzled.

"How strange! I wonder what –"

The classroom door burst open and Principal Kohn rushed into the room. Although he was usually immaculately dressed, today his tie was askew and his waistcoat unbuttoned. His pale face was covered with a sheen of sweat.

"What is the matter? What is going on?" Professor Feldman asked.

Principal Kohn held up his hands for silence.

"Girls, always remember March 19, 1944. This is a day of infamy in our country. The thunder outside these windows is the noise made by the approaching German army. The Germans have invaded our beloved country, and they are entering Budapest even as we speak." His face crumpled. "This is the beginning of very cruel times for the Jews of Hungary. I don't have to tell you how bitterly the Germans hate us." His voice cracked.

At the back of the room, Lina Weiszmann began to weep.

"As of now, the school is officially closed," Principal Kohn continued. "Your report cards will be mailed to you. I want you to go home singly or in pairs. If you go in groups, you may call attention to yourselves. Now I must dismiss the other classes." Principal Kohn turned at the door. "We can't do much about your uniforms, but please take the school crest from your berets before you leave," he added, closing the door behind him.

We were all dressed in identical dark blue pleated skirts and striped white-and-blue blouses with embroidered sailor collars. A dark blue beret with our school crest completed our uniform. The crest bore three metal letters – IGG – for the words "Israelite Girls Gimnazium." A safety pin held the metal letters in place, but it was easy to undo. Professor Feldman picked up a metal garbage can from beside his desk and passed it around the room. The crests dropped into it with a harsh clank.

After hasty hugs and quick goodbyes, I stopped in the doorway and looked at the scarred desks and chalky blackboard. How I would miss them! When would I see them again? I loved my school. I knew how lucky I was to be going to a high school that offered the chance of university. The entrance exams were so difficult that most of my friends had failed and had to attend technical school. I passed on my second try. There was also a Jewish boys' high school with equally high standards. These schools were our only chance: the regular state schools took very few Jewish students. You had to be a genius like my younger brother, Ervin, to be accepted into a state-run school. He was one of only two Jewish students in the fourth form of Kossuth Lajos high school, which was around the corner from our apartment.

Once we had descended the steep staircase to the street, Judit and I linked arms.

"What do you think will happen?" she asked.

3

I shrugged my shoulders. I was as frightened and confused as she was. We walked as fast as we dared. As we approached the Oktogon, at the crossing of Andrassy Street and Terez Ring, we were swallowed up by an excited crowd rushing in the same direction.

The perimeter of the gigantic plaza was ringed by rows and rows of cheering Hungarians. They were throwing flowers – daisies, lilacs, geraniums – at a long column of goose-stepping German soldiers in dark gray uniforms, long shiny boots, and peaked caps. The soldiers on foot were followed by hundreds more on gray motorcycles with sidecars. A long line of massive tanks brought up the rear. The conquering army circled the Oktogon over and over again. The onlookers were becoming more excited with each passing moment. They clapped, they laughed, and they showered the Germans with more flowers until they had covered the tanks in a rainbow of bright colors. Judit and I stood as if hypnotized while young women rushed up to the marching soldiers and hugged and kissed them. A man in a beret proudly lifted his toddler and passed him into the extended arms of a tank commander. I felt Judit tug on my own arm.

"Let's get out of here while we still can," she whispered.

Ten minutes later, Judit had turned down her street. Once I was on my own, I couldn't help myself – I ran until I arrived at our corner. For as long as I could remember, we'd lived in one of the old and elegant apartment buildings facing the Danube River, which separated Buda from Pest.

Papa's office was at the front of the building and our living quarters were right behind it, taking up the remainder of the first floor. Right across from our apartment house, on the wide rampart that separated the Danube from the road, I saw another long line of German soldiers, tanks, and motorcycles slithering alongside the river like a gigantic dark gray snake.

"Quite a sight, isn't it?" somebody said quietly at my elbow. It was Mr. Toth, the mailman. "The country is going to the dogs. To the dogs!" He spat with great precision in the direction of the conquering army. He handed me a large brown envelope with an official seal on it. "Would you please give this letter to your father, Marta?" he asked. "It's not something I relish giving him myself."

I ran up the worn stone steps. Mama flung open the front door before I even had time to take my key out of my pocket. She pulled me into her arms.

"They closed the school, Mama."

"Closed it? What do you mean? When will it open again?"

"I don't know. Principal Kohn told us they'll be mailing our report cards. Oh, I almost forgot. I saw the mailman outside. He gave me this letter for Papa."

When Mama saw the large, official seal on the envelope, her expression turned to ice.

"We must give this to your father immediately. I hope it's not . . ." Her voice trailed off.

"Where is Papa?"

"He is in his surgery, as usual," Mama said.

She knocked on the door of Papa's office. I had never seen her disturb him while he was with a patient. I followed her into the consultation room and recognized the patient immediately. Her name was Madam Emoke von Apponyi, but everybody always addressed her as Madam. She was the most famous dressmaker in all of Hungary. My mother was one of her clients before the war. Every year, Madam used to design an elegant new suit for Mama to wear to synagogue on the High Holidays.

My father tore open the envelope Mama had given him, read its contents, and without a word, handed it back to her. She read it, then crumpled the paper into a little ball that she clutched tightly in her fist. Tears filled her eyes. "Oh, Aron," she said.

Papa patted Mama's hand reassuringly, then squared his shoulders and gave a dry little laugh. "Well, my dear lady," he said to Madam, "you'll have to find yourself a new physician. It seems that I am needed in the capacity of a ditch digger in Yugoslavia."

I had feared that this moment would come. For weeks, we'd been hearing news of family friends who had been conscripted into forced labor regiments of Jewish men. My uncle Laci had been transported to the east. I had hoped that by some miracle, Papa wouldn't be called up. But miracles rarely happen.

6

"Oh, Papa! What will they do to you? When will you come home?"

He kissed my cheek but did not answer.

"I am sorry you've had bad news, Dr. Weisz," Madam said. Even though her features were set in their usual firm expression, I sensed that she was speaking from the heart. "Is there anything I can do to help?"

Mama cleared her throat. "Yes, you could help, Madam. I am an excellent bookkeeper. Perhaps . . . ?"

"I'm afraid I do my own books," replied Madam. "However, I can always use a fine seamstress."

Mama's face fell. "I can't sew."

"But *I* can," I said to Madam. "My grandmother taught me to sew beautifully. See?" With my heart hammering in my throat, I pointed to the intricately embroidered collar of my uniform. "I did that myself!"

Papa's face was an alarming shade of crimson. "Enough now, Marta. You must continue with your schooling!"

"The school has closed, Papa. What will happen to us while you are gone? And to Grandmama?"

"Don't be foolish, Marta," Mama said. "I'll get a job, even if I have to scrub toilets. We'll be fine."

Madam rose from her chair. The black silk dress she was wearing whispered formally as she smoothed it down with work-worn hands. She walked over to the door and stood for a moment with her hand on the doorknob. Then she tucked away an invisible lock of hair that had escaped the stranglehold of her chignon and stepped back into the room. She came up to me and touched the collar of my uniform.

"Fine work, Marta," she said. "You *are* an excellent seamstress."

She looked at Mama severely. "I hate to interfere in a family quarrel, Mrs. Weisz, but I am quite certain that you will have a great deal of difficulty finding a job in these times. It would be better for the child to work for me than for a stranger. At least I will be there to look out for her." She rested her fingers, rough with calluses, on my hair for a fleeting moment and gave me an encouraging nod. This was the first time she had shown me any affection in all the years I had known her.

"Please, Mama! Please, Papa!" I begged. "Listen to Madam! She knows what she is talking about!"

"Going to work is out of the question for you, Marta," Mama said. She turned to Madam. "Thank you for your offer. But you must not trouble yourself about us. I can take care of my family."

"Of course, Mrs. Weisz," Madam said stiffly. "Please remember that should the need arise, my offer will be open." Although she was addressing Mama, Madam was looking at me.

I didn't want to make my parents feel worse by crying, so I went to my private place – the landing at the top of a short flight of stone steps leading to the back entrance of our apartment block. The rays of the spring sun warmed my face. I was so absorbed in my wretchedness that a light tap on my arm made me jump. Peter Szabo was peering down at me in consternation.

"Marta, why are you crying? Tell me what's wrong, Shorty."

Even in my misery, I grinned at hearing my nickname. "Everything's horrible! I had the worst morning of my life. First, my school closed and then –"

"Come on, Shorty. I thought you hated school."

"But that wasn't the worst of it! When I got home, Papa received his conscription notice. He has to leave tomorrow morning to dig ditches in Yugoslavia." I could feel tears filling my eyes again. "What will happen to him? When is he going to come home? How will we manage without him?"

Peter sat down on the step beside me and put his arm around my shoulders. He let me howl until I couldn't cry any more.

"Good, you finally calmed down. Come home with me. You'll have to wash your face before you're a fit sight for human company. You don't want your parents to see you like this."

Peter lived on the fifth floor of our apartment building. When we were younger, Ervin and I spent countless hours at his place, playing dominoes or Snakes and Ladders on cold winter evenings. If the weather was good, we'd be on the sidewalk in front of our block, playing tag and hide-and-go-seek.

A sweet Liszt melody greeted us when Peter opened the front door of his apartment.

"Peter! Marta! How nice to see you, sweetheart," trilled Peter's mother, jumping up from the piano bench. "What are you two doing home at this time of the day?" She looked at my tear-stained face.

"We were let out early, Mother, because of the Occupation," Peter said.

I went to the bathroom and splashed cold water on my face and combed my hair. When I returned to the salon, I could see by Mrs. Szabo's frown that Peter had told her about my father. I sunk down into the comfortable sofa.

"Can I get you something to . . ." Her voice trailed off as a key turned in the front door. "Why, Dezso! I wasn't expecting you till much later. Look who –"

"Later, Agi! Later!" growled Peter's father, then he turned on his heels and left the room without greeting me. I was astonished because he usually made much of me, calling me his special pet and telling me how pretty I was.

"You must forgive Dezso his lack of manners, Marta. He has a lot on his mind. It's been difficult in the foreign office for him. But I mustn't say too much."

"Don't worry about me, Mrs. Szabo, I understand. Well, I should be heading home. I want to see Papa before –"

"Just a minute!" Mrs. Szabo disappeared into the kitchen. She came back with a parcel wrapped in a snowy napkin. "I baked poppy-seed rolls this morning. I know how much your father likes them," she said. "I heard they cut your rations again. I hope your poor mother will be able to manage."

I tried to give back the package. "Thank you very much. It's very generous of you, but I don't think my parents would want me to accept this."

"Nonsense, Marta," Mrs. Szabo said. "You know how close Dezso and I are with your folks." Peter's parents and Mama and Papa had been playing canasta on Thursday nights for as long as I could remember.

"Tell your father that I'll pop down later to say good-bye," Mrs. Szabo added as I was leaving the apartment. She made it sound as if Papa was going on a joyful vacation.

We woke up at dawn, even Grandmama Weisz. Although she usually lived alone in a cozy apartment on Rose Hill in Buda, she had come to us as soon as Papa phoned her with the terrible news. She wanted to be with Papa when he left.

"Look at all these glum faces!" Papa smiled at us with false cheer when we sat down at the breakfast table. A small vein throbbed in his temple. Grandmama's face was ashen, and Mama hid hers behind the coffee pot, her eyes red and puffy. She didn't even make any comment when I took some coffee. No one seemed to notice that Ervin and I were quiet. I was afraid I would begin to cry like Mama if I tried to talk. Ervin kept cracking his knuckles.

"Cheer up, Nelly," Papa said to Mama. He patted her hands, which she held tightly clasped on the tabletop in front of her. "I won't be gone for long. You'll see! I'll be back before you can even miss me!"

Mama buried her face in her hands.

"Aron, promise me you'll write often," Grandmama said.

"Every day, Mother. Every day. I promise," Papa said. "I want you to promise me something too, Mother. I am worried sick about you being all alone in your apartment. And with your heart condition and the extra expense with me gone . . . It would be so much easier if you moved in with Nelly and the children."

"I'd love to have your company, Grandmama," my mother added in an encouraging tone. "The children and I would be so much less lonely with you here."

Grandmama shook her head. "I don't know. What about my apartment? I can't just leave it and all my beautiful things behind."

"Mother, you know that Colonel and Mrs. Nagy would jump at the chance to rent it from you. They've been badgering you about it for years. They love the location." Papa was growing impatient. "Having you here, with Nelly and the children, would mean so much to me, Mother."

"Well, Aron, since you put it like that . . . I'll telephone Colonel Nagy later today to see if they're still interested." She smiled at Papa fondly.

He gave a sigh of relief. "Thank you, Mother. I'm glad that's settled. It was weighing on my mind. Nelly, you'll contact my patients? Let them know that I had to go?"

Mama nodded silently.

"Mrs. Szabo was going to come down to say goodbye. I guess something must have come up," I said.

Papa glanced at the grandfather clock ticking in the corner for a long moment, then stood up from the table. "Well . . . unfortunately, it's time for me to go."

We bade farewell in a sea of tears. When it was my turn to be hugged by him, Papa drew me very close and whispered in my ear: "You're like me, Marta: strong. Take good care of your mother and Ervin – and Grandmama."

I nodded as I felt my father's lips in my hair. Then Ervin claimed him.

Papa refused to allow us to accompany him to the railway station, but Ervin carried his knapsack down to the street. We crowded in the doorway to watch Papa's tall figure, slightly bent under the weight of the heavy bag, get smaller and smaller as he walked down the long avenue. Every few steps, he turned around to wave to us. Then, with a final wave, he turned the corner and was gone.

·2·

The Canary Yellow Star

H ow do I look, Marta?" Mama asked. She twirled in front of me.

"Very fashionable! Very pretty! I'd hire you for sure if you came to me for a job."

"I wish I could! That would solve all our problems," she said, laughing. She shrugged on a loden green coat. The April air outside was nippy. "My jacket is a bit threadbare, but it's still stylish, isn't it? I don't want to look shabby." I nodded my reassurance. "You did a wonderful job darning that nasty tear, dear." She held up her sleeve for my inspection. "The repair is barely visible. Well, wish me luck, darling!"

"Good luck, Mama! I'll stay home till you get back."

I spent the afternoon tidying up our apartment. I even went into Papa's office to dust his books. While straightening the papers on his desk and putting them into a neat pile, I uncovered an ashtray with a pipe in it. I picked it up and held it near my nose, inhaling its scent. I imagined Papa sitting at his desk, his pipe dangling precariously from the corner of his mouth, doing his paperwork after the last patient of the day was gone.

By the time I had helped Grandmama dust Mama's Herend figurines, delicate shepherds and shepherdesses frozen in perpetual happiness, dusk was falling. There was still no sign of Mama. I could see how worried Grandmama was by the way she kept peering into the darkness. Ervin repeated "Shouldn't Mama be home by now?" so often that finally I screamed at him to be quiet.

"You're too old for such outbursts," Grandmama admonished me. "A lady always keeps her temper."

We were so absorbed in our squabble that we didn't hear Mama come in. Her quiet voice startled us. "What's going on? What's the matter?" she asked. Her hair was disheveled and her tired face was smudged with dirt.

"You are so late! We were getting worried," Ervin cried.

I helped Mama pull off her coat. The red suit underneath was limp and stained. She walked over to the sofa and sat down. "I am so tired," she said.

I noticed that her nails were broken and dirty.

"Let me get you a cup of tea, Nelly," Grandmama said.

"Thank you, dear. That would be nice."

After a few sips, she seemed to revive. "Well," she said, "the good news is that I got a job. It wasn't easy. I took with me a list of the businesses owned by Papa's patients. I kept having snooty secretaries tell me that 'Mr. Magyar is in a meeting,' or 'Mr. Lakatos is out for the day,' or 'Mr. Peto is not hiring at the moment.' Finally, I got to Mr. Szabados's furniture warehouse, and I happened to meet him face to face. He would have passed me by as if he had never met me before, but I caught hold of his sleeve and stopped him," Mama said. She sounded angry.

"'I am Nelly Weisz, Mr. Szabados,' I told him. 'Don't you remember me? My husband was your physician.' The man had the grace to blush. Well, to make a long story short, I asked him for a job. After lamenting the sorry state of his business for several minutes, he told me that the only opening he had was for a cleaner in the warehouse. 'I don't think such a position would suit you, dear Mrs. Weisz,' he said. He was taken aback when I accepted the job. I was late coming home because I started immediately. It's dirty work, but I'll get used to it," she said cheerfully.

"Oh, Mama! A cleaner!" I couldn't imagine my glamorous mother doing such menial work.

"I'll leave school! I want to help," Ervin said.

"Don't even think about it!" Mama said. "There is nothing wrong with my job. It's honest work, and I feel lucky that I got a job at all. I'll be good at it. I have enough practice picking up after the two of you," she added.

"How much will they pay you?" Grandmama asked.

"That's the bad news. My salary is only eight hundred pengos."

"Oh, Nelly, what will we do? With all the inflation, I had to pay eighty pengos for a loaf of bread yesterday. We'll need at least two to three thousand to survive."

Mama ran her fingers wearily through her hair. "Well, Grandmama, we'll have to manage on eight hundred pengos somehow, because I can't get more."

"But I can! I'm going to ask Madam for a job."

"Absolutely not, Marta! I forbid it!" Mama said.

"Marta is right," Grandmama said. "We need the money she could be earning. We won't be able to manage without it."

"Please, Mama! Let me go to Madam's!"

My mother began to cry and drew me into a tight embrace. "Your father would be so angry! So disappointed!"

"Then we won't tell him."

"This isn't what I want for you, darling."

"I know, Mama. I know. But we have no choice. Once the war is over, Papa will come home, I'll go back to school, and everything will be as before."

The next morning, I was sitting on a straight-backed chair in Madam's office at the back of her salon on elegant Vaci Street. I tried not to rush my words.

"I came to accept your offer of a job, Madam. My mother was able to get work, but she is poorly paid. We can't make ends meet on her salary."

"Does your mother know that you have come to see me, Marta?"

"Yes, Madam. Mama knows."

"That's fine, then," Madam said. Her stern features relaxed into a half smile. "I am glad to see that you decided to take me up on my offer. You'll make a wonderful apprentice. Your salary will be twelve hundred pengos while you're training. More, of course, if you decide to stay on with me once you've finished the year. You will be responsible for sewing certain parts of my clients' garments. In addition, all the apprentices take turns cleaning up the workroom. Do you have any questions?"

"No, Madam."

"Good. You will start next Monday. Report to the workshop. The supervisor's name is Gizella. She will orient you. The apprentices all wear black dresses and white aprons. They use the back entrance." She glanced at me for a moment, then looked away. "There is something else, Marta." She shifted in her chair and tapped her fingers on the desktop in front of her. "You are the only Jewish girl in my employ. If anybody is unkind to you, please let me know. I'll take care of any problems."

I thanked her and stood up to leave. I was already at the door when she stopped me.

"Marta, what do you hear from your father? Is he all right?"

"We haven't had a letter for the past two weeks, Madam. Mama says he must be far from the mail or he'd write to us. The last we heard he was digging ditches near Bor. He said it was back-breaking work, but he was managing."

"Please send your father my best regards, Marta. I have tremendous respect for him." And she waved me out of the room.

A soft knock on my bedroom door. I sat up in my bed, still groggy from sleep. The door opened a crack and Ervin peeked into the room, beckoning me to get up. I rubbed my eyes and looked at the alarm clock by my bed. It was six o'clock in the morning.

Ervin was waiting for me in the parlor. He had a grim expression on his face and a white sheet of paper in his hand.

"Do you know what time it is?" I demanded.

"I got up early this morning to buy some milk at the grocer's before it sold out," Ervin explained, "and I found this announcement. It was tacked onto all the lampposts, to the front gate of our building, to the trees in the park." He was waving the paper in his hand. He seemed on the verge of tears.

"What's going on?"

"Read this!" he said, thrusting the sheet at me.

It was an official document, and I read it with growing dismay. It said:

> Attention All Jewish Residents of Budapest!
> As of April 5, 1944, every Jewish person six years of age or older must wear a ten-centimeter yellow star on his/her garments. The star may be made of cloth or silk or velvet. It must be properly secured to the left side of the clothing. Any Jews caught not wearing this badge will be immediately interned.

"I can't believe this. What does it mean?"

"What do you think it means? They want to isolate us, separate us, so that they can easily round us up," Ervin said. His eyes were full of despair.

"You're talking crazy! Why would they want to do that?"

"You've heard the same rumors as I have, Marta – that all the Jewish people in Poland and Slovakia were taken away to work camps, where they were killed by the Germans. It'll make it much easier for them to do the same to us if we are marked by yellow stars."

"Stop repeating such nonsense. Did you show Mama and Grandmama this announcement?"

"Mama has already left for work. Let Grandmama sleep. We'll tell her when she wakes up."

An hour later, my grandmother's lips whitened as she

read the paper. "We'll talk about this when your mother gets home," she said. "Don't leave the apartment unless it is absolutely necessary."

"What about school?" Ervin asked.

"Stay home today," Grandmama said firmly.

All day I read and reread the notice. No matter how many times I looked at it, I could not absorb the words. Why did we have to wear a yellow star? What would other people think about me when they saw me wearing it? I would be starting at Madam's next week. She said I was the only Jewish girl in her salon. How would the other apprentices react to such a humiliating badge? I worried and fretted like that until Mama arrived late in the evening. I could see by the expression of defeat on her face that she already knew about the decree.

Over dinner, Mama told funny stories about her job. We talked about how lucky it was that Ervin's school was still open, and I mentioned how nervous I was about starting work at Madam's. Everyone praised the delicious dinner Grandmama had cooked – green peppers stuffed with rice. We talked about everything – except the only thing on our minds.

Finally, Grandmama said, "So, Nelly, our government had a nice surprise for us today."

Mama's expression was grave. "I heard that the same thing happened in Poland. I was hoping the war would end before it was our turn."

"Mama, then you must also have heard what happened to the Jews in Poland! How they were taken away to work camps and murdered!" Ervin cried.

"Rumors," Mama said. "Alarmist rumors. Have you ever met anybody who was deported to a work camp?" she continued, without giving Ervin the opportunity to answer. "When I meet in person someone who was actually taken away, then I'll believe such rumors. Not a minute before."

"You're not listening, Mama. You'll never see such a person. The Jews taken to the camps are killed!"

"Are you trying to upset us?" Grandmama asked.

"You have to listen to me! I heard that –"

"That's enough, Ervin!" Mama said. "I don't want to hear another word of such talk." She turned to Grandmama. "Dinner was delicious, as usual."

"The best I could do without meat."

"I didn't miss the meat at all," Mama said. "I'll help you clear the table, and then, unfortunately, it's time to get to work."

After we had washed the dinner dishes, Mama went to her room, reappearing a few minutes later with her favorite silk blouse in her hand. It was such a pretty blouse – canary yellow in colour, with long sleeves and a tie at the neck. Mama had lent it to me several times for special occasions.

"Oh, Mama! Not your beautiful blouse!" I ran my fingers over the delicate material. It was so soft and smooth.

"It's the only yellow piece of clothing I own."

She took a pair of scissors out of her sewing kit and cut the blouse in half. Then she stretched out the material by pinning down its four corners.

"Let me make a pattern for the star," Ervin said. "Then we'll be able to trace its outline onto the material without making any mistakes."

He tore a page from one of his school notebooks and, using his ruler and a protractor, drew a six-pointed star on it. He then cut out the paper star and gave it to Mama, who copied its outline onto her blouse. She repeated this process several times, and then cut out the star figures from the yellow material with her sewing scissors.

"Come on, Marta, let's see just how skilled a seamstress you are," Grandmama said. She stitched one of the yellow stars onto the left side of her own jacket and another one onto Mama's coat. I sewed more yellow stars onto my coat, the uniform I would be wearing to work, Ervin's jacket and his school coat, and a couple of dresses my mother and grandmother often wore. I made sure my stitches were fine and small.

"That's enough," I said as I finished stitching the last star onto my favorite white blouse.

"What about your father?" Grandmama asked. "He'll need to have a star on his clothing when he comes home."

"You're right, Grandmama," Ervin said. "We have to be ready for Papa." He sighed. "I wish he would write us more often."

Mama and Grandmama exchanged worried glances.

"Your father must be far from the mail," Mama said. I could hear the anxiety in her voice.

"Which one of Papa's sweaters should I get from his bureau?"

"I'll get his green one. It matches his eyes," Mama said with a shy smile.

Within minutes, a yellow star had been sewn on Papa's sweater, ready for his return.

"Well, we're finally done," Grandmama said.

"Try on your jacket, Marta," Mama said. "Let's see how the star looks on it."

I put on my coat and turned around to model it for my family. They all stared at me, not saying a single word. Even Ervin, who never passed up an opportunity to make a sarcastic remark, was silent. I went into the foyer to look at myself in the full-length mirror that was hanging on the wall. Even in the dim light, the canary yellow star was ugly and garish against the navy material of my coat. The star felt heavy, as if it was made of lead instead of silk. I returned to the dining room.

"So what do you think, Marta?" Mama asked.

"It's not so bad," I said.

Early Monday morning, I approached the back doors of Madam's workshop for the first time. My heart was in my throat and my palms were wet. At the rusty metal doors, so different from the pristine wrought-iron gates that graced the front entrance, I joined a group of chattering girls hurrying into the building. They looked like penguins in their black dresses and white aprons. I saw them glance at the canary yellow star on my chest and begin whispering and giggling.

I followed the girls into the workroom. Fifty sewing machines were arranged in straight rows like desks in a school, and each apprentice sat down at her own station. A tall blonde girl, a little older than the others, stood at the front of the room.

"I am Marta Weisz, the new apprentice," I told her. "Madam asked me to report to you."

The girl looked me over, head to toe, her gaze resting on the yellow badge weighing down my heart. She was wearing an Arrow Cross pin, the emblem of the Hungarian Fascist party, on the collar of her dress.

"Jewish trash," she said, sneering. "Don't bother me!" She turned on her heels and walked away.

Somebody at the back of the room started to laugh. Another person hushed her. I stood staring down at the floor, not knowing where to turn, what to say, what to do. I could feel the heat burning in my cheeks. Finally, a small girl with a spotty complexion took two shoulder pads from a large bin in the corner of the room. She then went to a long metal coat rack that had dozens of blouses on hangers dangling from it. The girl pulled a hanger with a pink cotton blouse off the rack and returned to her seat. She proceeded to sew the shoulder pads into the blouse. I followed her example. I picked two shoulder pads from the bin and pulled a white lace blouse from a hanger. I looked around the workroom. A sewing machine in the last row was unoccupied, so I sat down at it and began to work. The girls around me were brimming with good cheer, chattering to each other. None of them spoke to me. It was as if I was invisible.

"My name is Marta," I said to a small redhead on my right.

"I am Magda," she replied in a cold voice and immediately turned to speak to her neighbor on her other side.

At home, I had no difficulty sewing shoulder pads into my dresses or Mama's suits. But somehow at Madam's, I had become all thumbs. No matter how hard I tried to sew the pads into the lace blouse, the shoulder pads ended up lumpy.

A gentle touch on my back startled me.

"Let me help you, Marta," Madam said, taking the offending object out of my grasp. I hadn't even noticed when she came into the room. "See? You have to smooth the pad down first, then pin it to the blouse. That way, it will fit neatly."

"I am sorry, Madam. I am usually not so clumsy."

"It's never easy to get used to a new place, to new circumstances," Madam said. Her voice was kind. She motioned to the blonde girl in the front of the room to come over to us.

The girl with the Arrow Cross pin hurried to Madam's side and smiled. "Yes, Madam?"

"Gizella, I'd like you to explain to Marta what she should be doing. Make her feel at home."

"I already did, Madam," Gizella said. She looked at me, daring me to contradict her.

"Fine, you may go then," Madam said. Gizella returned to her post, and Madam turned to me. "Come and see me in my office at the end of the day, Marta."

At seven o'clock that evening, I knocked on Madam's door.

"Come in and sit down. You look tired. Don't worry, the work will get easier as time goes by."

I sunk gratefully into a chair.

"How was your first day?"

"Fine, Madam." I wasn't telling the truth. The girls in the workroom had ignored me the entire day, but what was the use of telling Madam? She spent most of her time with customers and came into the workshop only a few times a day. What could she do? Order the others not to hate me? Not even Madam had the power to do that.

She looked hard at me. "I am glad to hear that everything went so well for you. How is your dear mama?"

"Fine, Madam. Working hard."

"Please say hello to her for me. Here, take these cakes home with you," she said, pointing to a plate of pastries on her desk. "I keep them around for my customers. They didn't eat everything I had put out for them."

She helped me pack them into a box.

· 3 ·

The Theft

All that spring, I trudged down to Madam's workshop on Vaci Street early in the morning. At first, every workday was the same as the one before, but in the middle of May everything changed. I was sweeping the workshop floor one day when Madam appeared. Fifty sewing machines fell silent. She announced that a staff meeting was to be held in the large salon at the end of the workday.

"I want all of you to be there," she said in a firm voice. And without another word, she left the room as abruptly as she had entered it.

"Oh no! Just like the old biddy! I have to meet Fritzi right after work. He is taking me to the movies. I can't be late," said Gizella as soon as the door was safely closed.

"I have a party meeting that I can't miss," announced her sister, Irma. She proudly fingered the Arrow Cross pin on the collar of her dress.

We began tidying up our stations. Madam was a stickler for neatness. Just a few scraps of material on the floor or spools of thread out of line were enough to anger her. I hurried to wipe the mirrors in the salon before the staff meeting. The elegant ladies who turned and dipped in front of them all day often left their fingerprints behind.

By the time I had poured the water out of the bucket, stored it in a closet, and hung the wet cleaning rag up to dry, the others were already milling about the salon. My right hand involuntarily sneaked up to my chest, where it covered the six-pointed canary yellow star on my black dress. But I told myself I was being silly, jammed my hands into the pockets of my apron, and plopped down on one of the crimson loveseats dotting Madam's elegant salon. The settees, loveseats, and armchairs were quickly being occupied. Some of the girls sat on the dark red Persian carpet covering the shiny parquet floor; others were leaning against the back wall. Soon all of the seats in the room were taken except for the one next to mine. Nobody sat down beside me.

Madam entered the room. Gravely, she looked from face to face. "I am sorry to keep you after work, ladies, but it was unavoidable." She noticed the girls standing by the wall and an angry expression clouded her features. It was gone so quickly that I thought I might have imagined it. "Why don't you ladies sit down?" she asked pleasantly. "You must be tired after a full day of work. Irma," she said to the girl closest to me, "there is an empty seat beside Marta. Sit down, please."

A mulish expression came over Irma's face. "I won't sit beside a stinking, dirty Jew, Madam," she announced. She looked around the room for the other girls' reactions. Most of the other apprentices were nodding their heads in agreement. Gizella was grinning. Two or three girls turned their heads away, careful not to look at me.

Suddenly, a strange sensation came over me. I felt as if I was watching a movie take place in front of me, and all the horrible things being said were about the Marta in the movie. The real Marta, me, was looking at this film and feeling sorry for her unreal, celluloid self.

"Silence," Madam thundered. Her voice switched off the movie in my head. She gave Irma an unpleasant smile that somehow reminded me of a black cobra getting ready to strike at her prey. "Marta does not seem dirty to me. Nor does she smell," she said in a reasonable tone. "Sit down, Irma," she repeated, pointing to the seat beside me.

Irma slunk over to the loveseat and sat down. She kept a space between us – no easy task, considering her size.

"As I was saying, ladies," Madam continued, "we have a problem." She walked over to a large mahogany cabinet holding bolts of the finest materials – midnight black woolens, snowy white linens, and silks in every color of the rainbow, all ready to be chosen by her wealthy clients. Madam had stockpiled the finest cloths before the German occupation. She unraveled a bolt of sky blue watered silk, revealing a large jagged edge where the material had been cut. "Can anybody tell me what happened here?"

Nobody spoke up.

She turned to Gizella. "Do you have an explanation for me?"

"No, Madam. We always cut the materials carefully, leaving a fine edge."

"When I saw this crooked edge, I measured the length of the silk," Madam said. "Four meters are missing. Four meters at sixty-five pengos per meter. I have been robbed of 260 pengos." Nothing like this had ever happened in Madam's salon. "The way I see it, I have two choices. I can either call the police or get the thief to return the material to me. I prefer the second course of action. It would be impossible to replace such fine silk with the shortages we're experiencing." She stroked the material lovingly.

"It's obvious that the Jew is the thief," Irma muttered.

"Madam, I didn't . . . I wouldn't . . ."

"Hush, Marta," Madam said. "I know you're not responsible. As for you, Irma, you'd better watch what you're saying!" With each word, Madam's voice rose higher and higher. She took a deep breath, then continued. "We may live in turbulent times, but I will not allow innocent people to be accused of crimes they did not commit. Indeed, I do not want to accuse any of you of being the thief. I have chosen a more civilized way to solve this problem," she said. We fidgeted under her scrutiny. Finally, she began to speak again. "This is what I would like you to do. When you get home tonight, each of you should make a bundle with old clothes or newspapers or rags – anything you want, as long as you have a bundle. Don't put your name on your package. The person who stole my silk should wrap up her ill-gotten gains. I want my silk returned tomorrow morning! If all of you leave your bundles in the salon, I will never know which one of you brought the package containing the stolen silk. I'll have my material returned to me, and everything can go back to normal. Do you all understand?"

There was a murmur of assent. Irma was staring angrily into the air. Gizella's hands were balled into fists and two spots of color dotted her cheeks.

"Irma is right! The Jew must be the thief, Madam. All Jews are thieves. Nobody else here would take your silk," Gizella said boldly.

"Gizella, did you not understand what I just said? I've had enough of your accusations. You and your sister had better watch your step!"

"You are the one who should watch your step, Madam! Be careful what you say to us. Our uncle is an important member of the Arrow Cross Party!" Gizella cried.

"Are you threatening me, Gizella? How dare you!" I had never seen Madam so upset.

Gizella became very pale. "No, Madam. I just . . . I mean, I'm sorry," she spluttered.

"Never mind what you mean!" Madam said. "I'm going to try to forget what you just said!"

"Thank you, Madam." The mutinous expression on her face did not match the humility of her tone.

Madam turned her back on Gizella and faced the rest of us. "That's all I have to say for now, ladies. Keep in mind what I told you: I expect to have my silk returned tomorrow." Her expression softened. "I am sure that by now, all of you must be ready to go home." And with a curt nod, she turned and left the room.

"Thieving Jew," Irma muttered as she brushed by me, jabbing me with her elbow. Both she and Gizella were gone before I could answer her.

The salon emptied quickly. A few of the girls cast furtive and sympathetic glances at me, but not a single one came over to speak to me. I told myself I didn't care, but I had never felt so alone.

The warm May sunshine blinded me for a moment as I stepped into Vaci Street. Many of the glamorous stores were boarded up, and yellow-star graffiti defaced the walls of the buildings. A dress shop on the corner was a pile of bomb-blasted rubble. A confectionery on the other side had become a large hole in the ground with a lot of debris piled up in it. I passed the window of Rozsi's Parfumerie, with its impressive display of crystal perfume bottles. On one side of a gigantic bottle of 4711 cologne was a sign stating: "If You Want to Smell Like Roses, Shop at Rozsi's." On the opposite side of the huge bottle stood a poster bearing a caricature of a swarthy, hook-nosed Jewish man with long, curly forelocks. Below the drawing was the word "Beware!" Next to the parfumerie was Olga's Patisserie, a welcoming café with cheery white tables that spilled onto the sidewalk. A sign affixed to the shop's doors warned: "No Jews or Dogs!" Lampposts bore signs warning customers to feel ashamed of themselves if they continued to shop in stores owned by Jewish people. Broken glass littered the street everywhere.

Most of the men wore uniforms, either of the Hungarian army or of the German SS. Some were accompanied by their well-fed wives. They were in sharp contrast to the few gaunt and shabby civilian shoppers, most of whom were women and old men. I was the only person wearing a yellow star.

I noticed three boys at the end of the street, laughing and shoving each other. The three were dressed in the uniform of the Arrow Cross Party – green shirt and red armband with a black insignia in a white circle. As I turned away from them, I walked straight into a boy behind me.

"Whoa!" he said, grabbing my arm. "You should watch where you're going!" He steadied me. My heart leaped at the sight of him.

"Peter, is it you?"

He laughed. "Who else?"

And then, suddenly, something strange happened. It was as if I had never seen him before, as if I was seeing him for the first time. I couldn't help noticing that scrawny little Peter had become a handsome boy – tall, with sandy hair, sparkling green eyes, and a friendly smile. He was wearing the familiar khaki uniform and peaked cap of the Levente. Jewish boys were discouraged from joining this paramilitary organization for youths.

"You look like a soldier in that uniform, Peter. Ervin should see you. He'd give anything to be wearing it!" Ervin was bitter that he wasn't allowed to learn how to shoot guns and march like a soldier beside his Christian class-mates when the troop met after school.

"How are you, Shorty?" Peter asked. "I haven't seen you for the past few weeks . . . too much homework. You look nice." He blushed fiery red. "How is Ervin? And your mother, grandmother?" he stammered. Suddenly, his eyes fastened on the canary yellow star on my dress. "What an idiot I am to ask such stupid questions," he said. "I should think twice before opening my mouth. Mother always says that I lack tact."

"No, no, that's fine," I reassured him. "You don't have to be careful with me. Just talk to me."

Peter smiled. "Have you got time for something to drink? There's a nice little place around the corner where we can talk."

I didn't know how to answer him. I wanted to go with him, but I knew I'd be in deep trouble if Mama found out that I went to a café by myself with a boy, especially a Christian boy, even if he was just a friend. I stood in indecision. Peter solved the problem by drawing my arm through his and starting off in the opposite direction to our apartment house.

We caused quite a sensation among the passersby. People glared at us as we walked down the street, and two young men in Arrow Cross uniforms blocked our path.

"Hey, you! You're a disgrace to your uniform, Jew lover," one of the men hissed, pointing his finger at Peter.

My heart was in my throat. I felt helpless and terrified and furious, just as I had felt back in Madam's salon. I wanted to scream, "Shut up! Shut up!" but by force of will, I kept silent.

"Scum!" Peter said angrily, pushing past them. "Ignore them, Marta!"

We hurried along, breathless with excitement. An old woman walking her dog stopped dead in her tracks, her eyes fixed on the yellow star over my heart. Suddenly, she leaned forward, grabbed my arm, and spat on the ground in front of me. I stared at her in shock until Peter pulled me away.

We finally reached the little Café Peace, which was tucked into the basement of a large building between a boarded-up furrier and a shoemaker. We were the only customers. Even the tiny, forlorn tables with stained marble tops did not look as if they belonged there.

Peter ordered two glasses of raspberry juice and we caught up with each other's news. It was so good to have a sympathetic ear. With my hands clasped in front of me on the rickety table, I told Peter all about my work and Madam and Papa in Yugoslavia. I also told him how worried we were that we hadn't heard from Papa for several weeks. I talked about our daily struggle to get enough food to eat. I mentioned the unfriendliness of our neighbors.

"Were you shocked by the way the people in the street were behaving? Everything is so horrible! I can't stand it any more!" I couldn't have controlled the torrent of words even if I'd wanted to. And I didn't want to. For some reason, it seemed important to make Peter understand what was happening to me. "I don't know why our friends and neighbors have turned on us," I continued. "We've never hurt them. I certainly haven't! Hungary is my country too! I was born here just like you, and so were my parents and grandparents. Grandpapa Weisz was even decorated in the Great War. I have as much right to live here as anybody!"

I tried to remain calm, but my voice was rising in anger and I was on the verge of tears. Peter patted my shoulder.

"I don't think it's a good idea for you and me to be seen together in public places," I told him. "It seems to upset everybody when they see that we're friends. That's why they make such cruel remarks."

"What about you, Marta? Do you still want to be my friend?" Peter asked. "That's all that matters."

I nodded. My mute answer seemed to satisfy Peter. He reached over and squeezed my hand.

"Would you like me to walk you home after work tomorrow? It'll give us a chance to talk," he suggested. "I'll give a call to Ervin too."

"You forget – our phone was taken away weeks ago."

"What a nuisance. I'll pop down to your place then. I'd have come before, but I've been studying for exams. I know how hard Ervin studies. He probably doesn't want visitors."

"Nonsense. He has to take a break sometime."

"You're right. So, Marta, do you want me to come for you at Madam's?" he repeated. He turned a violent crimson once again.

"I'd like that." A sudden shyness made it impossible for me to look at him. "Peter, don't tell anybody that we ran into each other – or that we're going to be meeting tomorrow."

"Why not? We're not doing anything wrong."

"Of course not. But you know Mama. Let's do it my way for now."

39

Peter looked troubled. "It doesn't seem right to me. But all right, I'll go along with you – just for now."

"Time to go!" I said, jumping up from the table and upsetting the flimsy chair I had been sitting on.

Peter and I walked home, and nobody saw us arrive together at our apartment block. I was glad.

I could smell the borscht as soon as I entered the apartment. Grandmama must have heard me come in, for she appeared in the doorway of the kitchen with a wooden spoon clutched in her hand. A large, flowery green-and-blue apron covered her neat navy dress. As usual, her hair was set in implacable gray waves, but she had loosened her collar in the warmth of the spring afternoon. I could see the heavy gold of the Star of David necklace that was usually hidden by her clothing. I was struck by how proud Grandmama was of her necklace and how ashamed we all were of our yellow stars. The necklace had been in our family for longer than anybody could remember. It was always worn by the oldest daughter. One day it would be mine, but not, I hoped, for a long, long time.

I was surprised when I didn't get my usual welcoming hug.

"Where have you been?" she snapped. "I've been out of my mind with worry."

"I'm sorry, but Madam asked me to stay late. It's a real nuisance not having a telephone. I don't like to call Mrs.

Marton with messages unless I absolutely have to." Mrs. Marton lived in the apartment right above ours. She had been a good friend in the past, but of late she had become more and more distant.

"Never mind that now," Grandmama said. "Never mind. Thank God you're home. Your mother hasn't come back from her sister's yet, and I don't know what to do about your brother. He got into some kind of a fight at school and won't tell me what happened. Try to talk to him."

My brother and I had become very close over the past few months. With Papa gone, and Mama and Grandmama more and more nervous as the days passed with no word from him, Ervin and I got into the habit of discussing our problems with each other. We soon learned that if anything went wrong, Mama would begin to cry and Grandmama would get chest pains. It was easier for us to rely on each other than to share our troubles with the adults.

I entered Ervin's room without knocking, ready to retreat if he decided to throw something at me. He was hunched over his desk, so absorbed in his writing that he didn't even look up. Crumpled pieces of paper littered the floor around his desk.

"Ervin, it's me! Look at me! What's the matter with you?"

"Leave me alone! Get out of my room!" he cried in a muffled voice, his back still to me.

I took a cautious step toward him. "Come on," I coaxed in a tone I would have used with a little child. "Come on! It's me!" I repeated. "You know I won't get mad at you."

Slowly, Ervin swung his chair around. I gasped when I saw his face. He had received a terrible beating. One of his eyes was swollen shut, his face was black and blue, his lips were twice their normal size, and streaks of dried blood decorated his forehead. I sunk onto his bed.

"I'm quite a mess, aren't I?" he exclaimed almost cheerfully. "Believe me, I gave as good as I got!" His battered face was proud.

"What happened? You promised Mama that you wouldn't get into any more fights."

"Well, you know, it was really unavoidable," Ervin muttered through swollen lips. "It started in geometry class. Old Nemeth returned our final exam today. I had only one mistake, but he gave me a C. I should have got an A. Sam Stein, who is the only other Jewish boy in the class, sits beside me. He had two mistakes, and Nemeth gave him a D.

"Pfeiffer was sitting in front of us, and I could see that his paper was marked up all over by Nemeth's red pencil. You know what an idiot Pfeiffer is. He's always getting into trouble and making a fool of himself. But the teachers are afraid of him because he wears his Arrow Cross uniform to class and his buddies are the Fascist bullies in the higher grades." Ervin sighed.

"Old Nemeth always reads everybody's mark out loud to the whole class. When he announced that Pfeiffer got an

A, I couldn't believe it! I put my hand up to ask him about my mark. He pretended not to see me. I was finally forced to address him without being called up."

"Oh no! You didn't!" I groaned.

"I had to, Marta. He just wouldn't call on me. I swear I was very polite. I said, 'Sir, could you please explain why Pfeiffer, whose examination is full of mistakes, received an A, while Stein, with two mistakes, was given a D, and I, with a single mistake, got a C?' Nemeth's face became so red that I thought he'd have a stroke. But no such luck. He only threw me out of the class."

"Oh, Ervin! How could you be so foolish? Mama's right: you look for trouble!" I wondered what Papa would have thought of Ervin. In my heart, I knew he would have been proud of him, but I also knew I shouldn't tell that to my brother.

"You're completely wrong, Marta!" he snapped. "I try to avoid getting into trouble, but in this case I had to say something. I just *had* to. Nemeth was so unfair. I kept asking myself why I should have to put up with such unfairness, such injustice. I wrote the better test, so I should have got the higher mark." He banged his fist on the table. "I couldn't stand it any longer! I've never done anything to them! I can't understand why they hate us so." He quickly wiped away the tears running down his cheeks. I pretended not to notice.

"Finish your story," I said. "You still haven't explained what happened to your face."

"There isn't much else to tell," Ervin said a little more cheerfully. "Sam was kicking me under the table to shut me up, and the rest of the boys were booing me in support of Pfeiffer." He shrugged his shoulders. "That just made me more angry. Old Nemeth hushed the class and started yelling at me, calling me an officious Israelite who shouldn't dare to compare himself to a fine Aryan boy like Pfeiffer. He sounded so idiotic that by then I didn't even care about his stupid mark." Ervin laughed, wincing at the pain from his cracked lips.

"Your face?" I interrupted, prompting him.

"Oh, that."

"Yes, that!"

"Well, after school ended, Sam and I were walking home. Just after Sam turned down his street, Pfeiffer and two of his Arrow Cross buddies jumped me and beat me up. They must have been lying in wait for me. But I put up a good fight! Pfeiffer has a bloody nose and one of his friends is missing a tooth. I could have got all three of them, but they had wooden planks. In the end, I had to run away. They wouldn't stop hitting me with the boards and calling me names. People passed us, but nobody stopped to help me." His face darkened. I thought of my dreadful afternoon in Madam's salon, but this wasn't the time to tell Ervin about it.

"Thank God you had the common sense to run away! They might have crippled you – or worse. But don't worry.

Everything will be fine in the end. Germany will lose the war, and then everything will be back to normal. You must learn to be more patient." My words sounded hollow even to my own ears.

"Stein meets with some older kids who are with the Resistance. You know what we've heard about the Jews in Poland and Slovakia? Those aren't rumors, Marta." He sighed deeply. "I don't want the same thing to happen to us. Look, I'll show you what I've been doing, but you must promise not to tell Mama or Grandmama. I don't want to raise their hopes."

"I swear!"

Ervin handed me a sheet of paper from his desk. It had a list of names and addresses on it. Then he picked up one of the crunched-up pieces of paper from the floor, smoothed it out, and gave it to me without another word. It was a letter, and this is what it said:

27 Andrassy St.
Budapest, Hungary
May 19, 1944

Dear Mr. and Mrs. Weisz,
I found your name in a New York telephone book in the central post office of my city. My last name, like yours, is Weisz. Do you think we might be distant relatives?

I am a fourteen-year-old Jewish boy who is afraid for his life. I live in Budapest, Hungary, with my mother, grandmother, and fifteen-year-old sister. My father was taken away to forced labor in Yugoslavia a couple of months ago. We haven't heard from him for a long time.

The German army occupied Budapest two months ago. Every day, new regulations are being issued against Jews. We can't go to high school or university or even get a job. We aren't allowed to have telephones, radios, or cars. We must sew a six-pointed yellow star onto our garments so we can be identified whenever we leave our homes. I've been getting beaten up regularly on my way home from school (although I always give as good as I get!). We are always hungry. We are desperate.

If you could find it in your hearts to sponsor us to come to America, I would do anything for you. You have my word on that. I would work for you twenty hours a day with no pay for the rest of my life, if that's what it took.

Respectfully yours,
Ervin Weisz
(P.S. I have enclosed an international stamp with my letter for your reply.)

"So what do you think, Marta? I found twenty-three people in the New York City phone book with the name Weisz. I wrote a letter to each one in my best handwriting. Do you think that one of these people might sponsor us to America?"

I was saved from having to reply by the sound of Mama's key in the front door.

Over the next few weeks, Ervin got up early every morning and rushed to the mailbox to check for replies to his letters. The mail delivery in Budapest was still quite regular in spite of the war, but no answers came to Ervin's letters. About a month later, all twenty-three were sent back stamped with a large black stamp: "Unable to Deliver. Addressee Has Moved to Unknown Address." Ervin shut himself up in his room for the rest of the day; he didn't even come out for dinner. He never mentioned his letters again.

"Go away!" I muttered, turning onto my side, eager to return to my dream. "I've got to catch the ball!" Once again, Ervin and I were back in Lake Balaton, both of us waist-high in blue water. Droplets glistened on our faces and bodies. The waves embraced us, tickled us, made us feel free. Papa was with us, a red beach ball in his hands. He threw the ball in our direction. I soared high into the air, as far up as I could, to catch it before Ervin, but . . .

"Get up! Something's happening outside!" Somebody was leaning over my bed and whispering urgently in my ear.

I sat up. The first thing I saw was Ervin's face. His swollen lips were twitching from excitement and fear.

"Come on! You've got to see this!" He motioned for me to follow him into his room. "Don't turn on the lights!" he warned.

Mama and Grandmama appeared in the doorway.

"What's going on?" Mama asked. "Do you realize it's two o'clock in the morning?"

"Shhh!" Ervin warned, his finger over his lips. "Something's wrong at the Weltners' apartment."

Ervin's window faced our building's courtyard, and the Weltners' suite was directly across from his room. He parted his drapes ever so slightly and we all peeked through the slit in the curtains. The lights were on at the Weltners'. We could see several figures moving about. Loud noises: the sound of broken glass and a scream. One of the figures fell down. Then a door slammed.

We ran into Papa's office as quietly as we could. The windows there faced the street, and we could see a long black car parked under the street light.

"Oh my God, the Gestapo!" Mama whispered.

"Oh no! Not Zsuzsi! Not Pista!" Grandmama said.

Three figures appeared on the street. When they reached

the street light, we could see that two men in dark suits and fedoras were escorting Mr. Weltner. The old man was dressed in pajamas, his feet in bedroom slippers. One of the men had grabbed Mr. Weltner's arm and the other was pointing a gun at his head. The two men pushed him into the waiting car.

Suddenly, old Mrs. Weltner came running out of the house. She was in her nightgown, her white hair flapping about her face. She was crying and begging the men to let her husband go. The man with the gun swung around and aimed, and a loud flash of fire lit up the street. The bang was deafening in the stillness of the night, but Mrs. Weltner crumpled to the ground without making a sound. The car sped away.

We were totally silent, afraid even to whisper lest a member of the Gestapo had stayed behind in the Weltners' apartment. Everyone in the block had suddenly become deaf and blind, and Mrs. Weltner's body lay untouched in a pool of her own blood on the moonlit street. When I finally risked sleep at dawn, I couldn't help feeling grateful that the Gestapo hadn't come for anyone in my family.

I arrived at the workshop a few minutes before eight the next morning, exhausted and nervous. Although it was still early in the day, the spring air was sticky and unseasonably hot. The gloomy skies seemed to echo the sight of Mrs. Weltner, lying crumpled in the moonlight.

Before breakfast, I had balled up several pages of an old newspaper and then covered the ball with another page of newsprint. Like me, most of the other girls had wrapped their bundles in newspaper. A few of them carried packages wrapped in rags. We all took our bundles – large, small, rectangular, cylindrical, round, or irregular in shape – into the salon before we went into the workshop. It was all done very quietly.

I spent the morning trying to make shoulder pads for ladies' blouses. It was difficult to concentrate, for I kept hearing in my head the deafening bang of the Gestapo gun. No matter how hard I tried, I couldn't make the shoulder pad I was working on less lumpy. To distract myself, I tried to think about Peter and how much I enjoyed his company. Unfortunately, this distraction didn't work. The latest shoulder pad I was making puckered more than ever. I tried to unpick my stitches and pricked my finger in the process. Now the shoulder pad was not only lumpy, but also had a bloodstain on it. It made me think again of the pool around Mrs. Weltner's lifeless body.

The workshop door opened and Madam came in. The sewing machines immediately ceased their monotonous song. I breathed a sigh of relief.

Madam's face was grave. She was carrying a bundle

wrapped in newspaper, but it looked no different from all the other bundles that had been left in the salon. She stood at the front of the room, facing our sewing machines and chairs, which were arranged in four rows, one behind the other. I was sitting in the last row by the wall. Madam looked at her employees for a long moment without uttering a word.

"Well, ladies, we have our culprit," she announced sadly. Slowly, she unwrapped the newspaper covering of the package she was holding and took out a rolled-up bolt of blue silk. She unrolled the silk and held it up for us to see. Clinging to the blue cloth was a scrap of yellow material, the exact same shade as the yellow star pinned to my uniform. All eyes turned to stare at me.

"I think it is very obvious who stole the material," Madam said.

"I knew it! I told you, Madam. It was the Jew! The Jew did it! I knew she was the one!" Gizella crowed.

"It was her!" Irma said, pointing her finger at me. "You can see it was her. A piece of her yellow Jew material stuck to the silk."

Automatically, I lifted my hand to hide the canary yellow star affixed to my chest. But as soon as I became aware of what I was doing, I forced myself to drop my hands into my lap. By now, the room had become silent.

"So, Marta, what do you have to say for yourself?" she asked.

"Madam, I did not steal your silk! Please, please believe me!" I pleaded, tears running down my face. "I wouldn't do such a terrible thing to you!"

"How do you explain the presence of this yellow material?" she asked, holding the scrap in her fingers and waving it in my direction.

"I can't explain it, Madam," I said. It was difficult to keep my voice calm. "I don't know where the material came from. I can only assure you that I've never seen it before. I swear that I did not steal your silk."

All eyes were still fixed on me. Madam, too, looked at me for a long moment before nodding almost imperceptibly. "Yes, Marta," she said in a much gentler voice. "I know you're not responsible for the theft. Let me show you what else I found, ladies." She carefully smoothed out the newspaper in which the silk had been wrapped and then held it up for all to see. It was the front page of a newspaper called *The New Dawn*, the mouthpiece of the Arrow Cross and the Germans. She held the newspaper by a tiny corner, as if it were dirty and she didn't want to touch it, then she let it fall.

"There are only two people in my shop who would read such garbage, such . . . drivel," she spluttered, "and neither one of those people is Marta. I am positive of that!" She pointed her finger at the Schulz sisters. "What you two have done is unforgivable. Stealing my silk was bad enough. Eventually, in these desperate times, I could have

overlooked that. But to blame your thievery on Marta —
that is beyond belief! It's totally reprehensible. You are
wicked girls!" she said. "You have ten minutes to gather up
your belongings and get out of my shop!"

"But, Madam, we didn't . . ." Irma pleaded. Gizella was
silent, biting her lips.

"Ten minutes!" Madam repeated. Her eyes never left
the offenders' faces. "I don't want to see either one of you
inside these four walls ever again," she said.

The Schulz sisters gathered up their belongings and
their pocketbooks. Irma scurried out of the room with her
head lowered, her eyes fixed on the floor. Her sister ambled
after her arrogantly, in slow motion. At the door, she
turned and, with an insolent smile, addressed Madam.

"You'll be sorry for what you just did, old lady! I can
guarantee you that!"

"Out!" said Madam. "Get out of here!"

With a shrug of her shoulders Gizella left, slamming the
door behind her.

I hurried home, eager to tell my family about the Schulz
sisters' deceit. Peter had a Levente meeting Monday nights,
so he couldn't wait until Madam had dismissed us. I found
my mother sitting at our kitchen table, staring into space.

"You're late, darling," she said. "I've been home for an
hour."

"Where is everybody? Is something wrong?"

"No, no. Everything is fine. Ervin and Grandmama walked over to Aunt Miriam's. She invited us for supper. I told her that we'd join them as soon as you got home. Come, rest for a minute."

I pulled up a chair. I noticed that she had picked the cuticles around her fingers raw.

"I am so dreadfully worried," she said. "No word from Papa or my parents . . . not even one letter."

"Don't worry. Papa is fine. So are Gran and Grandpa Schlamowitz."

Mama's parents lived in Miskolc, far from Budapest. The letters they sent us every week had stopped.

"There's only one other Jewish woman in the warehouse," Mama said. "She heard that the Jews in Miskolc have been sent to work camps. What if it's true? How could Gran and Grandpa survive?"

I took her hand. "You can't seriously believe that anybody would put old people in a work camp, Mama. They'd be useless there. Grandpa is too old to work and Gran has arthritis."

"I can't reach them, Marta," Mama said. "I've been writing to them every day and I never get a reply. That's not like them, not at all. If only they hadn't taken our phones away, I could try calling them." She looked desperate.

"Why don't you phone one of their neighbors, Mama?

They would probably be able to tell you what's going on. Mrs. Marton or Mrs. Szabo would let you use her phone."

"My clever, level-headed girl!" she said. "I can always count on you not to panic. I know that Marika is at home. I saw her come in when I was checking the mail. She was in such a rush that she didn't even stop to chat." She stood up. "Come on, let's go up to Marika's. I'll call the Varadis, who live next door to Gran and Grandpa. They've been neighbors for a long time."

We climbed the stairs to Mrs. Marton's apartment and Mama knocked on her door. No answer. I thought I heard footsteps coming closer, but nobody opened the door. Mama rapped loudly without success, then she rang the doorbell. The sharp sound reverberated in the stillness of the hall. A clock chimed inside the apartment, but there was no sign of Mrs. Marton.

"Marika must have gone out," Mama said. "Let's go up to Agi's."

We piled into the old-fashioned elevator with its wrought-iron walls. I felt like a bird in a cage whenever I rode in it. I pressed the button for the fifth floor. The sound of piano music wafted through the Szabos' front door.

"Oh, good," Mama said as she rapped sharply on the door, "Agi is at home."

The piano music died suddenly, but the door remained closed.

"I don't understand this," Mama said.

I rang the bell, then I beat on the door with my fists. I tried to look through the peephole, but I couldn't see anything. The apartment remained silent. Mama and I waited a few moments, then we tried knocking once again. No one opened the door. Finally, we returned home.

"Never would I have expected something like this of Agi or Marika," Mama said. "Not in a million years. I thought they were our friends."

"There must be some explanation," I said.

Mama did not reply.

Life at the workshop became more bearable after Irma and Gizella were fired. The other apprentices treated me with more civility than before. I still ate my lunch by myself, and nobody spoke to me unless it was about work, but the girls didn't call me names or threaten me like they used to. The Schulz sisters were becoming an unpleasant memory. Best of all, at the end of each workday Peter was waiting for me on the street in front of the salon, ready to walk me home. We walked together to the corner of our street, and I would wait until Peter got home before turning the corner myself.

But these happier days were not to last. When I arrived at Madam's shop on a sunny morning in June, the senior seamstress informed me that Madam wanted to see me in her office. I smoothed down my hair as best I could and knocked on her door.

After she called me in, she asked me to shut the door and sit down. I had known Madam ever since I was a little girl – first as Papa's patient and for the last months as my employer. I had seen her angry and upset, happy and satisfied. But what I had never seen was Madam frightened. The Madam in front of me was very, very scared. Her eyes were red-rimmed and swollen, as if she had spent the night crying.

She sat down behind her mahogany desk and waited a long moment before speaking. The silence in the room was broken only by the drumming of her fingers. Suddenly, she jumped up from her chair and rushed to the door. She opened it a crack and looked both ways down the hall before returning to her desk. Finally, she began to speak, but she was so quiet I had to lean forward to hear her.

"I am afraid I have some bad news, Marta," she stated. "Last night, I had some uninvited guests. Two men in a long, shiny black car appeared at my door. As soon as I saw them, I guessed who they were. The Schulz sisters were not exaggerating when they claimed to be well-connected. They reported me to the Gestapo . . . and you know what that means!"

She stood up and walked over to the window. With her back to me, she continued to speak. "I was told, in no uncertain terms, that if I do not fire you, they'll close down my business and deport me to the east." She stared out the window for a long moment, silent again.

"Fire me? But . . ."

When she turned around, I could see that she had regained her composure. She silenced me with a regal wave of her hand. Except for the tears filling her eyes, she was once again the imperious Madam I was used to seeing.

"I am so very sorry, Marta, but there is nothing I can do. If I lose my business, I'll have nothing left, nothing at all. I must do as they say." Her voice cracked with emotion.

I wanted to protest, but the right words wouldn't come.

She took both of my hands in hers. "We live in terrible times, and I fear that we have not yet seen the worst. Who knows where it will all end?"

I was so moved by her distress that I found myself trying to reassure her. I told her that she had already done enough for me, that nobody could have done more. She insisted on giving me an extra week's pay and promised that she would explain to Peter why I wasn't waiting for him when he came to walk me home at the end of the workday. But what surprised me most of all was how hard she hugged me when we said goodbye to each other.

· 4 ·

The Yellow-Star House

Mama was working the night shift, so I knew I'd have to face both her and my grandmother when I got home. They would be devastated when they heard that I had lost my job. My salary was necessary for our survival. Not even the strictest budgeting would make Mama's pay enough for both our rent and the inflated prices at the grocery store.

I saw that something was wrong as soon as I turned the corner of our street. A crowd had gathered around a poster affixed to the iron gates leading into our building. Many of the women were crying. I found Mama and Grandmama standing at the back, Ervin next to them. I wasn't surprised to see him at home – his state high school had recently thrown him out, along with the other Jewish students.

"Why aren't you at work?" was Ervin's greeting.

"I'll tell you later. What's going on?"

"Look," he said, pointing at the poster on the gate.

"I can't see what's written on it from here. What is it?"

"Three days! We have to move out in three days," Mama said.

Grandmama's hands were pressed to her chest.

"We have to move into a yellow-star house," Ervin said.

"A yellow-star house?"

"Our fair and wonderful government has decreed that all Jews in Budapest are allowed to live only in special houses marked by yellow stars. So we'll have to move," Ervin explained.

"That's not possible! We've always lived here! This is our home!"

"Read it for yourself if you don't believe me," Ervin said, pushing me toward the poster.

"Of course I believe you," I muttered. Still, I elbowed my way to the front of the crowd and read the notice. Ervin was right – we would have to leave our apartment in three days.

"Do you believe me now?" Ervin asked angrily. "The government decided which apartment buildings would become yellow-star houses," he said. "Ours was not one of them, so we'll have to move."

"Where will we go? We've never lived anywhere else. I love my room . . . my furniture . . . sitting on my window seat, reading. I don't want to go someplace different."

"We'll stay with Miriam," Mama said. "She sent us a message after you left for work this morning. Her apartment block became a yellow-star house."

"Does she have room for all of us?" Aunt Miriam, my twelve-year-old cousin, Gabor, and Uncle Laci lived in a three-room suite. Even with Uncle Laci gone, I couldn't see how all of us could stay with my aunt.

"A Jewish family is allowed to occupy only one room in a yellow-star house," Mama said. "Miriam will make space for us somehow. There won't be room for all our belongings, though. We'll take with us only what's absolutely necessary. Oh, it'll be so hard to decide what to leave behind. This is the only home I have ever shared with your father." She looked wistfully at the honey-colored stucco building behind us. The sad group of women and children dwindled. When I turned to go inside, Ervin caught my arm.

"First having to wear a yellow star, now this," Ervin said. "You wait and see, Marta. Before long, we'll be rounded up like cattle and deported to work camps like Grandpa and Gran."

"Shut up!" I cried. "Don't you let Mama hear you say things like that! Do you want to upset her even more? We don't know what happened to Grandpa and Gran. Stop imagining the worst! Even if they have been taken away, maybe the camps aren't such bad places." The week before, we had received a postcard from my mother's friend Ida, who was taken to a camp by the Waldsee in Austria. Mama's friend had written that she was working hard but enjoying her beautiful surroundings.

"Don't be so gullible, Marta!" Ervin said. "The postcards people get are fakes! The Nazis force prisoners to write them before killing them. Sam Stein knows. The Resistance knows."

"But it doesn't make sense. We are Hungarians. The government wouldn't let anything so terrible happen to us," I snapped. "I refuse to believe such foolish rumors even for a second. Mama told you to stay away from Stein and his crazy friends!"

"You're like everybody else," Ervin said. "Nobody will believe the members of the Resistance when they try to tell people the truth. I don't understand why."

There seemed nothing left to say, so we went into the courtyard. Grandmama was sitting on a wrought-iron bench by the staircase. I touched her arm.

"How will Aron find us when he returns home?" she asked. Her lips were white, her hands trembling. She looked much older than she had just a few short hours ago.

"If we're not here when Papa gets home, Aunt Miriam's apartment will be the first place he'll look for us," Ervin reassured her.

"Are you feeling all right, Grandmama?" I asked. "You're so pale. Let's go inside so you can rest."

Grandmama sighed. "Who has time to rest? But yes, let's go inside. I want to help your mother decide what to take with us to Miriam's."

We were tired and discouraged at the dinner table that night. Piles of our belongings were scattered throughout the apartment. It had been so hard to decide what to take with us when every object, every piece of furniture, had a precious memory attached to it. Even Ervin was too disheartened to do more than pick at the cholent Grandmama had cooked.

Grandmama's gaze swept across our glum faces. "I guess I'll have to try out new recipes. Nobody is eating," she said in a light-hearted tone.

"The cholent is wonderful, Grandmama," Mama said. She sighed and pushed away her plate. "All the happy memories . . . I can't bear the thought of leaving."

"My dear," Grandmama said, "we'll manage. Time will pass, and before you know it, Aron will be home."

"From your mouth to God's ears," Mama said.

Just then, the doorbell rang.

"Ignore it," said Mama. "I can't face visitors."

The doorbell shrilled again.

"I'll get it," I told her.

Peter was in the hallway, his face pale. He grabbed my hands. "I just found out you have to move, Marta. I don't want you to go."

"I don't want to go either, but we have no choice," I told him. I led him into the dining room.

"Peter, so nice to see you," Mama said. "Come, sit down."

He kissed both Mama and Grandmama on the cheek. "I'm so sorry you have to leave," he said. "Have you found a new place?"

"We'll be staying with my sister," Mama said.

"I want to help you move," Peter said.

"Thank you, dear, but I don't think that's a good idea. It's dangerous for you to be seen with us."

"I don't care. It's wrong that you have to go," Peter said. "It's not fair. I want to –"

The doorbell rang once again.

"See who it is, Marta," Mama said.

This time, I found Peter's mother in the hall.

"Mrs. Szabo, hello," I said, greeting her.

She brushed by me wordlessly and marched into the dining room. "Peter," she said, "come home immediately!"

"I'll be home soon, Mother," Peter said.

Mrs. Szabo turned to Mama. "Peter told me he is helping you move. How dare you put him in such danger! If someone reports him to the Gestapo, he will be deported."

Mama rose from the table and walked toward Peter's mother with her arms outstretched. Mrs. Szabo turned her head away. "Agi, it was Peter who asked to help us. Of course I refused his offer – not that I didn't appreciate it," she said, with a nod in Peter's direction. "I would not allow Peter to put his life in danger."

"Please let me help. I really want to," Peter said.

"It's out of the question," Mama said. She turned to Peter's mother with a smile. "Agi, come and join us for coffee. I'll miss you when we're gone."

Mrs. Szabo recoiled. She put out both of her hands as if to protect herself. I barely recognized her with her face so full of anger and hate. "I'm glad you have to leave! We don't want people like you around here! Good riddance!" she cried. Then she turned on her heels and left the room.

Although the June sun was beating down on our heads, I wore a long raincoat for the walk to Aunt Miriam's on Tatra Street. Mama had sewn all of her jewelry into the coat's hem, together with the little money we had left. We hoped the police and the roaming bands of Arrow Cross youths would be less suspicious of a young girl than an older woman. But I felt so sticky. Sweat was running down my face and my blouse clung to my back. Again and again, Grandmama's hand crept to her throat to feel the outline of her gold necklace. I whispered to her to stop.

It had taken us the whole three days to decide what to take with us. Saturday, June 24, was the last day of the compulsory move for the Jewish citizens of Budapest, so we couldn't hesitate any longer. I had used the last pengos I had received from Madam to buy a wheelbarrow from the super of our building for ten times its normal value. Even so, I considered myself lucky to have got hold of it. We filled it with our belongings, then tied two mattresses and several pillows and blankets onto it. Our family photographs rested inside the folds of the blankets. As we were leaving, Mama noticed the large silver menorah that had glistened on the sideboard in our dining room for as long as I could remember.

"We cannot leave this," she declared. "It was a wedding gift from my parents."

We tried to pack the menorah into the wheelbarrow, but it was so bulky that we had to take out the photo albums to make room for it.

"The photographs are more important," Mama said. And with that, the menorah went back on the sideboard. It was the last thing I saw when the door of our apartment closed behind us for the last time.

Ervin and I had each grasped a handle of the wheelbarrow and were pushing it in front of us in a wavering path. We'd also made huge rucksacks out of old sheets and then filled them with pots and pans, bedding, and clothing. Like beasts of burden, we bent under their weight.

The streets were filled with thousands of glum men, women, and children. Most people carried their belongings on their backs. A few were pushing wheelbarrows like ours. Others had larger, hand-held pushcarts. A few had been able to hire horse-drawn wagons. All of us had yellow stars sewn onto our clothing. We kept our eyes on the ground.

Because of our heavy loads and the crowded streets, the half-hour trip took three times as long as usual. Finally, we reached Aunt Miriam's apartment. She and Gabor were waiting for us outside. A large, six-pointed yellow star had been smeared above the front entrance.

"I'm so sorry we didn't come to help you move," Aunt Miriam said. "We were afraid to leave the apartment empty. There are people who couldn't find a room in a yellow-star house in this district and they've been demanding that I let them move in with me – even after I explained that you were coming! I'm so glad you're finally here. I don't know how much longer I could have held out. Gabor wanted to go alone to help you move, but I wouldn't let him out of my sight."

"Heaven forbid!" Mama said. "Who knows what might have happened to him. The streets are full of Germans, police, and gangs of Arrow Cross. It's a miracle nobody stopped us."

Aunt Miriam and Gabor lived on the third floor of their apartment house, but it took us just a few minutes to carry all of our belongings up the stairs. Once we had piled everything on the floor, we barely had room to move.

Even a steaming cup of Aunt Miriam's famous tea did little to revive us.

"We're terribly overcrowded," Mama said helplessly. "How can we . . ."

She exchanged puzzled glances with Aunt Miriam. Then they both laughed – the first time in ages.

"Where am I going to sleep?" I asked.

Neither answered: they couldn't stop laughing. But I was growing desperate. I *had* to know where I was going to sleep.

"I'm assigning rooms to everybody," I said. The only response was a snort and more laughter. "Mama, why don't you sleep with Aunt Miriam? Grandmama, you could take Gabor's bed. If you like, I'll keep you company. I'll sleep on one of the mattresses we brought with us. There is room for it on the floor by the door."

"She sounds just like Papa," Ervin said.

"My good, resourceful Marta. I couldn't manage without you," Mama said, drying her eyes on her sleeve.

"Good plan," Aunt Miriam said. "The boys can go into the parlor."

"Gabor, do you mind if Grandmama takes your bed?" Mama asked.

"Oh no! I prefer sleeping on the sofa in the parlor." He gave Ervin a worshipful glance.

"That won't be necessary," Grandmama insisted. "Gabor should stay in his own bed. I'll take the couch."

"I'd rather be with Ervin," Gabor said.

Ervin nodded happily.

"That's settled, then," I said. "We can pull Ervin's mattress into the parlor."

There was a final giggle from Aunt Miriam.

Once we had moved our belongings into the corners of the rooms, things seemed better. The apartment was still crowded, but at least we had space to move about. We even made a schedule for bathroom use.

The rest of the building was also a hive of activity. People were going in and out of the different apartments. Doors slammed. The cry of a child came through the wall. Ervin and Gabor went to help neighbors move while the rest of us unpacked what we could.

By suppertime we were tired. Grandmama had prepared bean soup and a spicy potato-and-noodle casserole with paprika. The delicious aroma made my mouth water.

"So nice to be together," my aunt said. "Now if only Laci and Aron were here."

"Just one letter," Mother said. "Just one letter – that's all I ask for."

"They'll write soon. They will, I know it!" Aunt Miriam's voice was determined, as if she were willing them to write to us. There had been no word from Uncle Laci either.

"Both of you worry too much," Grandmama said. She put her arm around Mama's shoulders. "I'd know if anything was wrong with Aron. I'd feel it. Aron is fine, and so is Laci."

The three women exchanged unhappy glances.

"Are there other kids our age on this floor?" I asked Ervin.

As if in response to my question, the doorbell rang. I went to answer it. Judit Grof and her brother, Adam, were standing in the hall.

Judit and I stared at each other in complete shock before falling into each other's arms.

"What are you doing here?"

"We moved into Mr. Deutch's apartment down the hall," Judit said. "I had no idea I'd find you here! We just came over to introduce ourselves."

"And I didn't know you'd be here! Isn't it wonderful? We'll be able to spend all of our time together."

I drew her into the apartment and we settled down on the sofa.

"Careful! You're in my bedroom," Gabor said, laughing. "I feel cooped up. Let's go out!"

"Great idea! We've been moving all day. I want to have some fun," Judit said.

"It's such a nice evening. Let's go for a walk by the river," I suggested.

Aunt Miriam's apartment was around the corner from a

wide promenade that ran alongside the Danube. Before the Occupation, we went there often. The cafés by the river sold delicious ice cream and pastries, and lively music wafted out of the hotels. White wooden deck chairs were rented out to people who gazed for hours on end at the romantic sight of the Royal Castle and the Fisherman's Bastion across the river. Throngs of chattering people of all ages strolled up and down the wide walkway. The air was filled with the tantalizing aroma of the pretzels the street vendors were hawking.

"We can't go on the promenade! It's too dangerous," Gabor said.

"Gabor is right. The entire area is full of Arrow Cross, SS, and Hungarian soldiers," Aunt Miriam explained. "You won't see a single yellow star in the crowd."

A heavy silence oppressed us.

"It was a lousy idea anyway," I finally said, as cheerfully as I could. "Who wants to see the murky old Danube again? I've seen it a million times already and so have the rest of you. How about playing cards instead?"

Mama gave me a grateful glance. "What a good idea," she said. "We'll leave you in the kitchen and drop over to Judit and Adam's apartment to visit their mother."

I was cutting thick slices of heavy rye bread for breakfast when I heard somebody banging on the front door. I found Adam in the doorway, a ripped white notice in his hands.

"I was playing catch with my friends when the police tacked this on the lamppost out front," he said. "I tore it off and took it to my mama. After she read it, she told me to show it to you." He handed it to me and turned away.

It was an official document, a new set of rules and regulations that Jewish citizens living in Budapest had to follow. I read the announcement with growing dismay. A curfew had been imposed. We were now allowed to leave our homes only between two and five o'clock in the afternoon. We weren't permitted to have guests come to our homes. We could not call out of our windows to friends, even if they happened to live across the street from us. We could not use the same air-raid shelters as Christians. We were not allowed to sit on park benches. We could not visit the homes of Christian acquaintances, even if they lived in a yellow-star house. Most humiliatingly, we were allowed to travel only in the last car of a streetcar, even if the other cars were empty. A Jewish person caught disobeying these regulations faced immediate deportation.

I took the poster to Mama. As she read it, her expression became more and more grave.

"As if wearing a yellow star isn't humiliating enough!" Her voice broke. "How are we going to live?"

I shrugged my shoulders. I could only wonder how I would ever see Peter again.

Despite the new regulations and his mother's threats, Peter sent me a note asking me to meet him at the Café Peace. Although it was a sunny July afternoon, I took along a sweater with no star on it. Just before I got to the café, I would put it on to hide the yellow star on my blouse, since Jews were forbidden to eat in restaurants. Both Peter and I knew the risk we were taking. So far, we'd been lucky: no police had come into the café to check papers. But we knew that our luck couldn't last forever. We were going to have to find another place to meet.

I had told Judit my secret. I was certain she wouldn't betray me, for behind my loyal friend's practical exterior beat a romantic heart.

"Peter must like you a lot," she said as I was dressing.

"Of course he likes me. We've been friends for ages."

"You know what I mean." She giggled.

"Don't be silly! He's just a friend. I've known him forever." I could feel the heat rising in my cheeks, a sure sign that a blush was about to follow.

"So what if you've known him for a long time? What's that got to do with anything?"

"So . . . so nothing! Nothing at all! We're just friends," I repeated, though I knew it was not true.

When I'd finished dressing, I said goodbye to Judit and told Mama I was going out to buy some food. I told myself I wasn't really lying to my mother, just postponing telling her the truth. Still, I felt so guilty when she accepted my explanation with no questions asked. Food shortages had become so severe that my excuse was believable. We were allowed fewer rations, and we could not go to the grocer's early in the morning because of the curfew. By the time we did get to the shops, the shelves were bare; most of the day's merchandise had already been sold to customers who were able to line up early in the morning. Sometimes it took hours to find a grocery store that could sell us a loaf of bread or a small block of cheese.

"Be careful," Mama said as she looked me over from head to toe. She didn't ask why I was wearing my one good skirt. Its black folds ballooned out satisfyingly and made my waist seem smaller. Grandmama had made it out of the dress I used to wear at Madam's. My former apron had become a fashionable white blouse with a Peter Pan collar. A wide black belt completed my outfit. I didn't own any high-heeled shoes, so I had to be satisfied with my ancient, slightly scuffed black Mary Janes. I had asked Judit to take a piece of charcoal from the stove and draw two straight black lines down the back of my legs. From a distance, it looked like I was wearing nylon stockings with seams. I had rolled the front of my hair into a fat sausage curl, just like the one the American movie star Judy Garland wore. In the bottom of my only purse, a hand-me-down from Mama, was Judit's lipstick. It was Passion Red. She lent it to me whenever I went to see Peter. I knew better than to try to put it on at home, however. Mama would have killed me.

74

Once I was out the door, I quickened my step. The streetcar was clattering to a stop at the end of our street just as I got there. I climbed up into the last car, but it was full, so I had to stand. At least I knew I wouldn't smear my charcoal seams against the seat. I put the strap of my purse over my shoulder, shifted my sweater into the crook of my arm, and with my other hand, clutched the leather loop hanging from the ceiling. It bothered me that I still had to stand on my tiptoes to reach the loop, but I was afraid to hang on to one of the metal poles next to the seats. I wasn't in the mood for nasty comments about how I was crowding the passengers in the seats next to the poles.

There were two other people with yellow stars in the last car. One was a white-haired lady who was sitting with a large wicker shopping bag on the floor between her feet. A few seats over from her was a youngish woman with a little boy in her lap. The blond child steadily picked with his chubby fingers at the yellow star on his mother's blouse. The only sounds came from her fruitless attempts to hush her little boy's chatter. The rest of the passengers seemed absorbed in their own thoughts – all except an older gentleman who was hanging on to the last leather loop at the back of the car. He was dressed rather formally, in a black suit with a black homburg on his head and a briefcase clutched in his hand. He smiled at me.

At the first stop, two youths wearing the green shirts of the Arrow Cross climbed aboard. The first boy stopped close to me and grabbed one of the leather loops hanging from the ceiling. I inched away from him as inconspicuously as I could. His friend walked up to the old Jewish woman and kicked her wicker basket with his filthy boots.

"Hey, mother!" he sneered, spitting on the lady's shoes, "why is a dirty old Jew like you taking up my seat? Get the hell up!"

The old woman hoisted the heavy basket over her arm and stood up wordlessly. The youth pushed her aside and lowered himself onto her seat with a laugh. The lady shuffled down the streetcar to where I was standing. None of us in this compulsory society of the yellow star looked at each other. Not a single one of the other passengers betrayed any sign of noticing what had just happened. It was as if the lady was invisible.

We arrived at the next stop. Two policemen in their distinctive blue uniforms climbed the steps of the streetcar. My heart pounded when I saw revolvers in the holsters on their hips. The older of the two policemen remained by the back exit while his younger partner came to the center of the car. Two more waited on the sidewalk by the streetcar rails.

"Your papers, Jews!" cried the younger policeman.

I was glad I had remembered my wallet. I took out a card that bore my picture and information about my age, sex, and address. Across the card was stamped the word "Israelite." The policeman went up to the lady with the basket first. He checked her papers and flung them back at her. Next, he came to me. He examined my documents, nodded, and returned them. I breathed a sigh of relief.

"Both of you, get out!" the policeman said, pointing first to the older woman and then to me.

I was confused. "Why, sir? My papers are —"

"Are you arguing with me, Jewish bitch?" the policeman shouted.

"No, sir, I was just —" I stopped mid-sentence. The lady with the basket had kicked me hard over my ankle while she stared impassively out the streetcar window. To my great relief, the movie in my head switched on, just as it had back in Madam's workshop. Once again, I was watching events unfolding around my other self.

"You what?" the angry policeman prompted me.

"Nothing, sir," the girl in the movie mumbled.

"Cat got your tongue?" the policeman snarled, pushing his face into mine.

The movie dissipated like smoke, and I was back in my unbearable real world. The officer grabbed my arm and pushed me down the steps of the streetcar. The old lady with the basket stumbled down close behind. Two more policemen were waiting for us on the sidewalk. As I stood, terrified, I could see and hear everything that was happening inside the streetcar.

The younger policeman had approached the woman with the little boy in her lap. For a moment, the woman sat frozen. Then she put her child down on the floor, pulled her identification papers from the pocket of her dress, and handed them over to the policeman only after he repeatedly shouted at her to do so. The child clung to his mother's knees, looking in turn at her white face and the beefy policeman looming over her. The boy began to suck his thumb.

The woman's papers showed that she was from Gyor, a town two hours away by train. She did not have the documents necessary for living in Budapest. The woman apologized and told the policeman she would be applying for her Budapest papers immediately. She explained that she had arrived in the city only a few hours ago. But the policeman ordered the woman off the streetcar with her child. She must have realized that being caught without her documents meant deportation. She got down on her knees and begged him to let her and the child go.

The policeman grabbed the woman's arm and pushed her toward the steps. The child was still clinging to her skirt. The older officer, who had been guarding the exit, rushed up to the petrified little boy, tore him away from his mother, and carried him down to the street. The child began to wail. The mother, who had been kicking and clawing at the younger officer, gave up her fight and ran down the steps to reclaim her child. She grabbed the boy out of the policeman's grasp and clasped him tightly to her chest, stopping right next to me.

"Why you . . . !" the policeman thundered. He drew his gun out of his holster and aimed it at her head. The woman covered the child's eyes with her hand. My own eyes were riveted on the policeman's fingers, which were moving toward the trigger.

"I'm sorry to interrupt, sir, but you forgot to check my papers." A quiet, dignified voice broke the tense silence. The man with the briefcase was climbing down the street-car steps. "I am also a Jew."

The officer lowered his gun. "Halt, Jewish dog!" he cried. "Where is your yellow star?"

"I am not required to wear one," the man said. "My documents, sir." He held out his papers to the policeman. Below the rim of his hat, his forehead was beaded with sweat.

"God bless him," the mother of the child whispered under her breath.

"All right, Jew, let me see your papers," the policeman growled, putting his gun back into its holster. His three colleagues exchanged relieved glances while he began to examine the man's documents. "Is this a joke? What is this?" he asked. The other officers crowded around him, murmuring to each other.

"Where did you get this?" another one of the policemen asked. All of the officers seemed very interested in the Jewish man's documents.

"I have a Schutz-Pass. A Swedish protective passport," the man said in a calm voice. "It was given to me by Mr.

Raoul Wallenberg, from the Swedish embassy. Hungarian authorities do not have jurisdiction over me any longer. I do not have to wear a yellow star. I am a Swedish subject, a Swedish citizen protected by Sweden. You must let me go."

"He is telling the truth," said one of the policemen, his voice laced with amazement. "This Jew has some kind of Swedish passport. We have to let him go."

"Damn it, you're right!" said one of his colleagues.

None of the officers was looking in our direction. "Run!" I whispered to the people standing next to me. The woman with the basket dropped her load; the mother picked up her child. All three of us raced away. As we turned the corner, we scattered in different directions.

I ran and ran. I ran until I had no breath left to run any more. The entire time I kept thinking, Who is this Wallenberg? What is a Schutz-Pass? How can I get one?

I was afraid to get on a streetcar again, so I alternately ran and walked the rest of the way. By the time I arrived at the Café Peace, I was an hour late, hot, sweaty, and totally exhausted. Would Peter already have left?

I forced myself to stop for a moment to regain my breath before descending the well-worn stone steps to the café. A few minutes earlier, I had slipped into a public bathroom to splash some cold water on my face. Nobody was around to see me emerge with my hair neatly combed and my white sweater buttoned up to the chin, covering the yellow star on my blouse. I wasn't able to see the back of my legs easily, but my seams appeared not to be smudged. I had also put Judit's lipstick to good use.

Peter was sitting at a corner table sipping raspberry juice and looking anxious. The sudden delight that filled my heart at the sight of him made me feel shy.

"Thank God you're finally here. I was worried sick when you didn't come," he said.

"I was scared that I'd missed you, that you wouldn't wait." Peter's response was a wry lift of his eyebrows that made me feel much happier. I collapsed into a chair. "Let me rest a couple of minutes, then I'll tell you what happened to me."

Peter ordered a glass of raspberry juice for me. I drank it greedily and felt much better. Then I told him everything that took place on the streetcar. "Who is Raoul Wallenberg? Have you ever heard of him?" I asked.

"No, but my father might have," Peter said. "I'll ask him."

"Please don't tell him I'm the one who wants to know."

"Of course not. I know I can't tell him. Does your mother know you're here?"

"No. I want to tell her, but I'm scared."

"Why? We've been friends for ages."

"How about these reasons: you're not Jewish, and it's dangerous."

Peter sighed. "What do you want to do today, Marta? Do you want to go for a walk?"

"Let's do something else, something that's really crazy. I am so sick of the war. I just want to have some fun." I thought of the young woman and the frantic child.

Peter laughed. "Fine. We'll do whatever you want."

"Do you really mean it?"

"Of course. Just tell me what you want to do."

I didn't have to think before answering. "I want to go dancing. I even know where I want to go – the Casino on Margaret Island."

Peter paled under his tan. "Marta, we can't. I was at the Casino with my parents last week. The show doesn't start until nightfall, long after your curfew. If you are caught by the police or the Gestapo, do you realize what will happen to us?"

I knew very well – the threat of deportation loomed large. But I didn't care. For once, I wanted to forget about the war. I just wanted to enjoy myself. "We won't be caught. I feel lucky tonight."

"It might be dangerous." Peter looked worried.

"You promised. You said you'd do whatever I wanted to do. I guess you didn't mean it."

Peter groaned. "Of course I did, idiot that I am. All

right, I'll go. But I want you to know that it's not the sensible thing to do."

"I'm sick of being sensible," I told him. I jumped up and pulled Peter out of his chair before he had a chance to change his mind. He sighed resignedly and followed me out of the café.

Twenty minutes later, we were on the number 6 streetcar as it bounced over the bridge to Margaret Island in the middle of the Danube. I had never been to the island, a beautiful park full of hotels, theaters, outdoor swimming pools, and cabarets. When the streetcar stopped in front of the Casino, just past the bridge, we got off. The Casino was the most elegant and popular dancehall in the entire city. It was also a jazz lover's paradise, especially if you were lucky enough to get a garden table.

We entered the tall white building through wide-open wrought-iron doors. A plump, white-haired maître d' in a black tuxedo greeted us solemnly.

"The young lady and gentleman require a table?" he asked. Peter and I stood up a little straighter, and I moved closer to Peter.

"Two for espresso," Peter said, taking hold of my hand. "We'd like to be seated in the garden."

"The garden is full," the man replied frostily.

"Are you sure?" Peter asked. We could see through the double doors that only half the tables were occupied. Peter reached into his pocket, pulled out a few folded bills, and slipped one into the maître d's hand. "Could you check your book again, please? Just to be sure."

The older man put the money into his pocket. His smile became much friendlier. Puffing up with self-importance, he leaned over his reservation book again. "Ah yes! Let's see if we can do better," he said. "Yes, I believe we can! Table 4 seems to be available."

"I thought it might be," Peter said, winking at me.

The maître d' turned to me. "May I hang up the young lady's sweater? It's a warm evening."

"No!" I said much too loudly. I crossed my arms across my chest protectively.

Peter put his arms around my shoulders and squeezed. "She's always cold, even on the warmest day," he said, laughing.

The maître d' nodded and held up a finger. As if by magic, a young waiter appeared beside him. "Sanyi, my boy, take the lady and the gentleman to table 4," he commanded.

We followed the waiter into the beautiful dining room with its parquet dance floor. Huge marble columns entwined by ivy stood in a row across the center of the room. Several of the tables set out between the columns were empty. Most people preferred to be outside on such a warm evening. Peter and I crossed the long dance floor to our table. It was in a perfect spot, just a few feet from the band. The evening program had not yet begun. I felt very grown up when the waiter pulled out my chair. Peter sat next to me.

"Quite a place, isn't it?" he whispered with a smile.

"Just beautiful!"

"Do you require menus?" the waiter asked, his tone only slightly less supercilious than that of the maître d'.

"No, thank you. We'll each have an espresso, please." I was certain that even a cup of coffee would be expensive in this place.

"We'll also have chestnut pudding with whipped cream," Peter said to the waiter, ignoring my kick to his ankle.

"Are you crazy? It'll cost a fortune," I said as soon as the waiter was gone.

"Don't you like chestnut pudding?" Peter asked.

"Of course I do! But it's too expensive."

"Let's not worry about expenses tonight," Peter said. "Let's forget about the war for a while."

Most of the men dining around us were in uniform. A group of Arrow Cross officers at the next table smiled at us, and we smiled back. I could not help thinking how a small hidden star on my blouse would erase those smiles.

The band appeared on the stage. After a few minutes of screeching, mooing, and tuning their instruments, they were joined by a singer. She was wrapped in a sparkling blue cloud from head to toe and her white teeth were gleaming against her flawless, tawny skin. She was the first

Negro I had ever seen. She seemed so alive that I couldn't take my eyes off her.

"She is from America," Peter whispered.

The singer snapped her fingers once or twice and broke into a spirited rendition of my favorite Ella Fitzgerald song, "A Tisket, a Tasket." I couldn't understand the English lyrics, but I recognized the tune immediately. The hot jazz beat was so infectious that I tapped my feet to the rhythm.

Peter grabbed my hand. "Let's dance," he said.

Our jerky, rhythmic steps were a perfect match.

"Where did you learn to swing like this?" Peter asked.

"Oh, here and there," I said mysteriously. I wasn't about to tell him I had been practicing with Judit every afternoon. It helped to pass time during the curfew. "What about you? Who taught you to dance?"

"My parents entertain a lot. I took lessons. I have to know how to dance."

For the next few hours, I swam in music and happiness. We danced and danced, and between dances we talked, savored the chestnut pudding, and washed it down with several cups of strong, sweet espresso coffee. As darkness fell, the waiter lit the lantern in the middle of our table. The pinpoints of light did a lively little dance of their own on the snowy tablecloth.

At ten o'clock, the music changed to the romantic "Moonlight Serenade." The vocalist announced that it was the last song of the evening, and Peter pulled me very close. I rested my head on his shoulder as we swayed to the plaintive harmony. I thought I could feel his lips against my hair, but I wasn't sure.

Suddenly, Peter danced me into the dining hall. We stopped behind one of the marble columns in the embrace of the ivy. My heart was beating so loudly that I was certain he could hear it. We stood for a long, long moment, looking at each other wordlessly. Slowly, he bent down and kissed me on the lips. I pulled back.

"Marta, I –"

"Shhh," I said. Then I kissed him back.

· 5 ·

Shabbos Dinner

We made our way home from the dance without meeting a single member of the Arrow Cross, the Hungarian police, or the German army roaming the streets. I was afraid to take a streetcar, so we walked the entire way. It was past eleven o'clock when we arrived at Aunt Miriam's. The street was deserted and eerily dark. Even the moon had hidden behind the gathering clouds. A storm was in the air. All the street lights had been turned out and the windows, though open to the stifling night, were draped in dark black-out curtains because of air-raid regulations. I could barely see the smeared outline of the yellow star above the doorway.

"Well, here we are," I whispered sadly. "Thank you for a very special evening. I had a wonderful time." Much more than that, sang my heart.

"Me too," Peter said. He was standing very close to me,

88

his breath fanning my face, his arms on my shoulders. I was hoping he would kiss me again. "Marta," he stammered, "back at the Casino . . . I've been wanting to tell you for a long time —"

The gate creaked open before he could finish. He jumped back a step.

"Is that you, Marta?" It took me a moment to realize it was Mama. "Is that you out there?" she repeated. "It's so dark I can't be sure."

"Mama! What are you doing here? I'm not alone. Peter Szabo is with me."

"Mrs. Weisz, hello!" Peter said.

A horrible moment of silence followed. "Say goodbye to your friend, Marta," Mama said. "I'll wait for you inside."

The gate to the building clicked shut behind her. There was just enough time for Peter and I to squeeze hands before I followed her into the courtyard.

"What have you got to say for yourself, Marta?" she asked. Although her voice was low, I could hear her fury. "I knew by the way you were acting that you were up to something. Sneaking around with Peter like some kind of . . . tart. How could you? I expected more of you! What have you got to say for yourself?"

I didn't answer.

She grabbed my arm and shook it. "Do you realize what you're doing? The boy isn't Jewish. You could be killed. *He* could be killed. Shame on you!"

I remained silent.

"And not telling me . . . You wouldn't have dared to behave like this if your father was at home!" She slapped me across the face with a heavy hand.

I was so shocked that for a moment I couldn't speak. I just stared in her direction in the darkness, my hand protecting my face. Neither of my parents had ever hit me. Tears began to pour down my cheeks.

"We weren't doing anything wrong. I'm only fifteen, Mama! For once I wanted to have a good time. We went to the Casino for one of the tea dances."

The corner of Mrs. Grosz's blackout curtain lifted even though both of us were whispering.

"A good time! A *good* time! Don't you realize you could have been transported for breaking the curfew? For associating with a Christian boy? Didn't you realize what a chance you were taking? Didn't Peter?" Suddenly, she began to weep. She pulled me close to her. "The Szabos can't be any happier about this than I am," she continued. "We were such good friends, and look at us now. They made it clear where their sympathies lie."

"Peter isn't like his parents, Mama."

She let go of me and sighed. I wanted to see her expression, but the darkness obscured it. "Let's go upstairs to bed," she said finally. "We'll talk tomorrow."

I undressed in the dark as quietly as possible and tried to put Mama's anger out of my mind. As I lay on my mattress on the floor, next to Grandmama's bed, I relived every enchanted moment of the evening that had just passed. I could feel Peter's arms around me, his lips moving in my hair. Once again we were swaying to "Moonlight Serenade." Peter was kissing me, and I was kissing him back. Then I fell asleep.

The next day, Mama asked me to go to the greengrocer's with her. "I may need help carrying the potatoes," she said.

"We'll come too," Ervin volunteered. He and Gabor were playing chess at the kitchen table.

"No need," Mama said. "I probably won't be able to buy enough potatoes to make it worth your while. Marta's help will be more than sufficient, and I'd welcome her company."

Ervin gave me a knowing look. I wondered if he had been awake when I got home last night. The parlor where he was sleeping faced the courtyard.

As soon as we reached the street, Mama took hold of my arm and pulled me over to the side of the building. "I owe you an apology, Marta," she said stiffly. I could sense the effort the words took. "I couldn't sleep all night. I can't believe I actually hit one of my children. I'm very sorry. There is no excuse for it, but I was beside myself." She sounded so tentative, so humble, so unlike her usual proud and confident self that my heart filled with love and pity.

"Forget about it. I have. I'm sorry you were so worried."

"I can't help weeping when I remember my own fifteenth year – the parties, school, friends. Then I see what you have – the scrounging for food, the way we live, the constant fear. And Papa! Not knowing where he is, how he is . . ."

She looked so sad that I tried to console her. "It's not so bad, Mama. We've got each other. And Papa will be home soon and the war will be over." I sounded much more optimistic than I felt.

"From your mouth to God's ears," Mama said. I was glad to see that she was able to give a slight smile. "Peter . . ." she said. "He's not just a friend any more?"

I could feel myself start to blush. Mama looked searchingly into my eyes, and I returned her look, unblinking. That exchange of glances made us into equals, two women sharing a precious secret.

Mama patted my face gently. "The boy isn't Jewish, Marta! I know he's a good boy, and I am fond of him. But he isn't Jewish," she repeated, as if I needed reminding. "You're a young lady now. This is not what I want for you, my first born, my only daughter! In normal times I would forbid you to see this boy, but nothing is normal nowadays." She sighed deeply. "I can see that Peter makes you happy, and happiness is a most precious commodity. So tell me everything."

And I did. I told my mother everything . . . well, not quite everything. But I did speak about the abuse we had received from people on the streets when they saw us together. I even told her how I started covering up my yellow star whenever we went out in public. Mama was horrified.

"Marta, you mustn't be so reckless! If you're caught, you'll be deported. So will Peter! Promise me that you won't do anything so foolish again," she begged. She grabbed my hand and squeezed it so hard that it hurt. "We must obey their rules if we're to survive. If we disobey them even a little bit, we're lost. There are just too many of them – and they have guns! There is no way we can defy them. Surely you must realize that!"

"I'll be very careful, but I *will* see Peter if I can. He is decent and kind and he makes me feel alive. Can you see that?"

"I'll try, but it won't be easy," Mama said, gathering me into her arms. "I'll try."

I laughed weakly from relief.

"No daughter of mine will sneak around with a boy behind my back," Mama added, her voice full of the old authority. "Invite Peter for Shabbos dinner. Ask him to be careful not to be seen entering our apartment. And don't worry about explaining the situation to Grandmama and Aunt Miriam. I'll talk to them."

What had I let myself in for? And Peter – I knew he liked my family, but how would he react to being cross-examined by them? They could be extremely nosy. To stop my imagination running wild, I decided to change the subject and tell Mama what had happened on the streetcar. I told her all about the mother and child who did not have the proper documents, and about the old Jewish man with the Schutz-Pass that had been given to him by the Swedish diplomat Raoul Wallenberg.

"The man said the Schutz-Pass protected him. It made him into a Swedish citizen. Neither the Hungarians nor the Germans can touch him. The policemen on the streetcar were about to let him go when the rest of us ran away," I explained. "Peter is going to find out from his father about this Mr. Wallenberg and how we can get his Schutz-Pass to protect us."

"But, Marta, his father —"

"Don't worry! You can trust Peter. He won't tell his father that we asked him to get this information for us."

For the first time in a long time, I saw a glimmer of hope in Mama's eyes.

"Marta! Come and help me set the table," Mama called from the kitchen. "Your guest will be arriving in half an hour."

I adjusted the collar of my blouse and gave my hair a final pat in front of Aunt Miriam's old-fashioned dresser. As I stood in the kitchen door, I heard Mama and Aunt Miriam arguing.

"What were you thinking of, Nelly? Why in the world would you invite Peter here?"

"Miriam, it means so much to Marta. Nothing we do seems to matter anyway. She might as well have an evening to remember."

When they saw me, they stopped talking. Grandmama was at the stove, bent over a large cast-iron pot, stirring a mysterious concoction.

"Yummy smell! Are you finally going to tell me what we're having for dinner?" Although I'd begged and begged, my grandmother had refused to tell me in advance what she was planning to cook for Peter's visit. She said she wanted to surprise me.

"Come, have a taste," Grandmama said, dipping her wooden spoon into the pot.

The surprise turned out to be my favorite casserole, made with slices of green pepper, rice, onions, tomatoes, and salami. Of course, there was no salami. But Grandmama had somehow managed to get the vegetables at the greengrocer's and had made a secret substitution for the meat. It tasted exactly the same as when we were still able to get all the ingredients. I was certain Peter would like it.

My mother was standing at the kitchen counter, stacking up the dishes I was to use to set the table. Grandmama always insisted that we use our best dishes on Shabbos, and the kitchen table was already covered with Aunt Miriam's second-best tablecloth. I snuck a furtive glance at Mama as

I piled the crockery into my arms. To my relief, she forced a smile and winked at me when she noticed I was looking at her. I knew I had been forgiven for the night at the Casino.

"Hurry up, Marta!" she said. "Your guest will be here in a few minutes."

I forced myself to concentrate on the task at hand. The kitchen table was crowded, but it looked beautiful. Aunt Miriam's white-and-gold Rosenthal china, crystal glasses, and silver cutlery sparkled in the rays of the setting sun. Two heavy, ornate silver candlesticks graced the center of the table. I folded snow white linen napkins into the shape of fans and set them behind each plate. They gave the table a festive air. I kept praying under my breath: "Please, God! Let everything go smoothly."

All at once, the doorbell rang.

"Peter's here!" Mama called. "Get the door, Marta!"

I took off my apron and, after a last-minute glance at my reflection in the window, went to let him in.

Peter was standing in the corridor, a large package under his arm. I was glad of my white blouse and black skirt when I saw his eyes flicker over me and his smile grow even broader.

"You look very pretty, Marta," he said. "I missed you," he added in a soft voice that the women in the kitchen couldn't hear.

"Me too," I whispered. "You look nice too," I said in a louder voice. And he did, in his gray pants, white shirt, and green necktie. It made him look older – at least eighteen.

"Any problems getting here? It's a real nuisance that you have to sneak around to visit us." I had warned Peter that if our building's nosy super stopped him, he should say he was visiting Mrs. Kocsis, a Christian lady on the fourth floor.

"No problems at all. I didn't see anybody. Here, this is for you." He handed me the package he was holding. "I couldn't get you flowers, so I brought you this instead."

The parcel contained a large loaf of black rye bread and some butter. I couldn't even remember the last time I'd had butter with my bread. Peter must have been saving his ration coupons for weeks to obtain such a rare commodity. Both Mama and Grandmama were suitably impressed, and Mama's guarded expression relaxed slightly.

"This is very generous," she said, looking at Peter's gifts on the kitchen counter. "So generous that we mustn't accept it. I can guess how many of your coupons you must have saved up to buy the butter, not to mention the bread."

"Please, enjoy both the bread and the butter. It's for you." Peter's ears were bright red. "I didn't need the coupons. I found someone who . . . I mean, I traded some coupons with him. That's all."

Mama's face softened. She patted Peter's arm. "You're a good boy," she said. Both Grandmama and Aunt Miriam were smiling. I knew then that everything would be all right.

"Well, then," Mama said, "thank you. We'll enjoy your generous gift tonight." She cut thick slices from the bread and transferred the butter into a pretty little dish. Then she put both the bread basket and the butter on the kitchen table.

Although my family was not terribly religious, we lit Shabbos candles every Friday night. Ervin and Gabor put black satin yarmulkes on their heads. My mother, grandmother, and aunt covered their hair with silk scarves, but my own head was bare, since I was the only unmarried girl at the table. We all crowded together while Grandmama lit the candles. Her hands moved over the dancing flames as she chanted an age-old Hebrew prayer: "Blessed art Thou, Lord our God, King of the universe, who sanctified us by His commandments and commanded us to kindle the Sabbath light."

I murmured the prayer along with her, praying for the war to be over, for Papa to come home. For my Gran and Grandpa to return. For Uncle Laci to come back. And for Peter to like me – a lot.

Soon Grandmama was dishing out her casserole and Mama was handing around slices of the bread Peter had brought. We spread it sparingly with butter. For a while, we concentrated on our food, but Mama's words broke the silence.

"So how have you been keeping? How are your parents?"

"Mother and Father are very well, thank you," Peter said. "Father's been busy . . ."

"He works side by side with the Germans?" Mama asked.

"I am afraid so," Peter replied, his eyes fixed on his plate. "I myself would not, but Father won't listen to me."

"It's not your fault," Mama said, patting Peter's hand.

A sudden silence engulfed us. I couldn't think of a single word to say to ease the tension around the table. Finally, to my great relief, Ervin broke the silence.

"How often does your Levente troop meet? Do you know how to use a rifle yet?" He tried to sound casual, but he kept cracking his knuckles, a sure sign he was nervous.

"We meet three times a week for an hour, right after school. Mondays and Wednesdays we practice marching and athletics, and learn the rules of guard duty," Peter said. "There is also a meeting on Fridays for target practice."

Ervin's expression reflected the envy he was feeling.

"Friday is also the day for political discussions," Peter added with a grimace. "They're compulsory."

Ervin shot Gabor a quick glance. "We couldn't join the troop at school," he said. I recalled the black eyes my brother and cousin had sported after they'd tried to take part in this paramilitary training. "I don't suppose we could join your troop?" His hands were fidgeting.

Peter's ears turned a brilliant shade of crimson. "There is nothing I'd like more," he said. "But I don't think . . . I can't . . ." His voice trailed off miserably. He took a deep breath before continuing. "The truth is that several boys in my group are also in the Arrow Cross. They ganged up on poor Alex Schwartz when he tried to get in. I don't know what would have happened to him if my friends and I hadn't stepped in to help."

The warmth around the table vanished. Peter was glumly examining his plate. Ervin, staring at him angrily, was clenching and unclenching his fists. Gabor was biting his lips, not looking at anyone.

"Well, if you don't want us to . . ." Ervin began in a challenging voice. I knew it was time to interrupt him.

"Don't be ridiculous. It's not Peter's fault you can't join the Levente. In any case, this certainly is not the time to discuss it!"

"Marta is right. Let's talk about more cheerful topics," Mama said.

Ervin nodded reluctantly, although I could sense that he was still angry.

"How is school? What are you planning to do after you graduate?" Aunt Miriam asked Peter in a bright voice.

"Go to university, then join the diplomatic service, if they'll have me," Peter said modestly. "What about you, Marta? What do you want to do?"

"I just want to go dancing," I told him. Peter glanced at me, then looked down at the table. I bit my lips to prevent myself from laughing when I saw that his ears had turned bright red once again.

"Come on, Marta, be serious!" Ervin said. "I want to be a doctor like Papa!"

"Ah! How nice. Both of you boys want to follow in your fathers' footsteps," said Aunt Miriam.

"I don't really care what I am studying, as long as I can go to school," Gabor said. "I miss it."

So did I. Although I used to complain about homework and our teachers, now I wished I could see my friends and even mean old Professor Feldman. I missed the excitement I used to feel when I learned something new. I even missed the scarred desks and the smell of chalk.

Silence fell over us once again. All of us were thinking the same thing. Papa became a physician like his father before him, and ever since he was a little boy, Ervin had been saying that he wanted to be a doctor just like Papa. Now Papa was somewhere in Yugoslavia digging ditches, and Ervin, Gabor, and I could not go to high school. The difference between Peter and us was like an ocean. He had a future; we did not. The unfairness of it all almost overwhelmed me. But it wasn't Peter's fault. I looked at my mother beseechingly. She and my aunt were on the verge of tears. When I turned to Grandmama, she squared her shoulders and nodded encouragingly.

"Well," she said, "doesn't anybody like my casserole? Why isn't anybody eating?"

We laughed in relief and dug in once again.

The moment had come for me to ask. "Peter, did you speak to your father about that Swedish official, Wallenberg?"

"My father didn't know much more about it than what you had already told me, Marta," Peter said. "Papa says that Raoul Wallenberg is a low-ranking Swedish diplomat who arrived in Budapest last month. Mr. Wallenberg has been issuing Swedish passports at his embassy on Gyopar Street in Buda ever since he arrived. Father also said that Mr. Wallenberg has been giving these Schutz-Passes to Jewish people who have some kind of connection to Sweden – relatives there or business dealings, anything like that."

Peter stopped for a moment to take a drink of water. The rest of us stared at him, our mouths open, forks suspended in the air. "Mr. Wallenberg claims that neither the Hungarian government nor the Germans have any authority over these people. Jewish people with Schutz-Passes are protected by Sweden. They don't have to wear a yellow star." He shook his head incredulously and chuckled. "What's most amazing of all is that both the Hungarian government and the Germans are accepting these documents as completely legal. Any Jewish person who is given a Schutz-Pass by Mr. Wallenberg is safe for the time being."

It took a moment for us to digest Peter's words.

"We must get these Schutz-Passes somehow," Mama said.

"But we don't have any connection to Sweden," Aunt Miriam protested.

"We'll find one," Mama said in a determined voice.

"My late husband, God rest his soul, was in the furniture business. I think he imported lumber from Sweden," Grandmama said.

"Do you think that's enough to get us our Schutz-Passes?" Aunt Miriam asked.

"It will have to be," Mama said. The three women exchanged hopeful glances.

"Marta," Mama said, "you'll wear your white blouse tomorrow with your black skirt. I want you to look your best."

"Are we going to the Swedish legation, Mama?"

"Of course we are. The minute the curfew is over."

.6.

The Schutz-Pass

The next morning, Mama and I set out for the Swedish legation on Gellert Hill in Buda. We had to walk. The last car of each tram that went by was already crammed with star-marked men and women. The other cars were half empty, but they were forbidden to us.

It took us more than an hour to climb the steep hills to Gyopar Street. The Swedish embassy was halfway up the hill. It was a gracious honey-colored villa surrounded by a tall wrought-iron fence with sharp spikes on top. When we reached it, we were caught up in a sea of frantic and shoving men and women with yellow stars. Desperate men were trying to climb the fence. Harried guards kept the iron gates locked, opening them a crack to let in a few at a time from the front of the queue.

Mama and I elbowed our way into the center of the

agitated, tense crowd. The heat and pressure of the bodies around us took my breath away. We clutched each other. A woman in front of me shrilled over and over again: "My uncle lives in Stockholm! Let me in!" Beside me, a man yelled at the top of his voice: "I export paprika to Sweden! I need a Swedish passport!" Mama was becoming so pale that I was afraid she would faint and be trampled.

"This is impossible! Let's go home!" I shouted in her ear.

We elbowed our way back out of the crowd. Mama's carefully pinned hair was tumbling down over her shoulders and our clothes were rumpled. Mama was on the verge of tears, and there was a lump in my throat too. I put my arm through Mama's and we began the long trudge back down the hill. We were on the steps leading down to the river when the sirens began to scream.

"My God! An air raid!" Mama cried.

I cupped my hands over my eyes to look up into the sunny sky. It was clear of airplanes, but the sirens kept on wailing. "We've got to find a shelter!" I said.

"Where?"

We both knew that we were only allowed to use the shelters in yellow-star houses. And even in those houses, the safest spots, the ones along the basement walls, were reserved for Christian tenants. We hadn't passed any yellow-star houses on our way to the Swedish embassy.

Now the street was filling up with people. They were leaving their homes and heading for a tall, official-looking building at the end of the street. Several people carried suitcases or backpacks. A man had a mattress on his back. A teenage boy was clutching an ugly little white dog in his arms to prevent the yelping puppy from running away. A little girl was dangling a birdcage from her hands. The yellow budgie in it was hiding its head under its wings.

At the entrance of the tall building, an old soldier barred our way. Something seemed oddly familiar about him, then I realized he was dressed in the same uniform from the Great War that Grandpapa Weisz had worn. His photo flashed in front of me — it used to be proudly displayed on top of the piano in my grandmother's apartment on Rose Hill.

"Get away from here, Jewish filth!" The soldier slammed the door in our faces.

A huge bang. A building exploded in a funnel of fire at the other end of the street. We ran in the opposite direction, taking refuge under a canopied iron gate leading to the garden of a villa. The bombing continued. The smoky stench of the fires made my nose twitch and my eyes burn. A large smoke rectangle appeared high in the sky. As soon as I saw it, I realized that American bombers were hiding high above the clouds and carpet bombing was about to begin. The first missile fell with a loud whooshing noise.

"What are we going to do?" Mama cried. She sounded frantic.

"Let's go to that apartment house," I suggested, pointing

to a large building on the other side of the street. "They'll have a shelter for sure."

"They won't let us in!" Mama said, touching the yellow star over her heart.

Before she could stop me, I grabbed the yellow material and tore it off her dress. Then I ripped my own star off my blouse.

"Marta, are you crazy? If they catch us, we'll be transported!"

"If we can't get into a shelter, we'll be killed! Let's go!" As I grabbed hold of her arm and pushed her toward the building, I noticed that the black stitch marks where the star had been were still visible. We had to make them disappear.

"Dear God, what are we going to do?" Mama wailed.

I ran into the rose garden behind the canopied gate, crouched down, grabbed a handful of dirt, and rubbed it over the front of my shirt. Then I scooped up more dirt and smeared it over the front of Mama's dress. We were both filthy, but the outlines of the stars were gone.

We ran across the street into the tall building. Arrows painted onto the walls directed us to the entrance of the air-raid shelter. The door of the shelter was locked from the inside. We banged and banged until our knuckles hurt. The din outside was growing louder by the moment. Just then, the door opened slightly and a black eye peered out and looked us over. The owner of the eye opened the door wide.

"Come in! Hurry up! It's dangerous out there!" he commanded.

We ran down the worn stone steps. The apartment house's bomb shelter, which was also its basement, was full of people. A bare light bulb in the center of the room lit the tense faces. Every inch of floor space was occupied. People were standing in groups or sitting on the cement floor quietly talking to one another. A woman was crooning to a baby in her arms. Mama and I sat down quietly on the floor near the exit, careful not to call attention to ourselves. We held hands tightly for comfort. Although I was very frightened by the bombing, I was also glad to hear the explosions. Every bomb the Americans dropped meant the war was coming closer to an end and Papa would soon be coming home.

A middle-aged man with a brown beret sidled up to me where I sat on the floor. I slid farther away from him. The man came even closer until his leg was pressed against mine.

"Hey!" he whispered.

I turned my face away and tried to ignore him.

"Hey!" he repeated, pushing something into my lap. I looked down and saw that it was the jacket of his suit. "Put on my jacket to cover that star!" he whispered urgently.

I looked down at my blouse. I saw that the dirt had flaked off my shirt and the outline of the six-pointed star was again visible. Fortunately, Mama's was still covered by earth. I shrugged on the man's jacket and buttoned it with shaking fingers. Just then, there was a tremendous bang outside. The building shook mightily and the lights went out. I hid my face in Mama's shoulder. A child began to wail, and a woman at the back made a wild keening sound. Finally the all-clear signal sounded and the lights flickered on again. I turned to my neighbor to thank him, but he was gone. I wore the jacket home.

One afternoon a few days later, I had the apartment to myself. Grandmama was resting and the others had gone to look for groceries. I lay on my mattress, eyes closed, luxuriating in the silence. The sound of the doorbell made me jump. When I looked through the peephole, I saw it was Peter. I recognized the red-headed boy standing beside him. He had gone to school with Ervin, but I couldn't remember his name. I swept the door open.

"Marta, nice to see you," Peter said. "Do you know Sam Stein?"

"Ervin has talked about you," I told him. He was not wearing a yellow star and I could see how nervous he was by the way he kept tapping his foot.

He looked around the room. "Is Ervin home?"

"Nobody is here except my grandmother and me. And she's having a nap. Everybody else is at the grocer's. They should be home soon, however; the curfew will be starting shortly."

"I would have preferred to talk to Ervin, but we'll have to tell Marta instead," Sam said to Peter. "We can't stay here until he gets home. They're waiting for us."

Peter nodded and turned to me. "I won't tell you more than I absolutely have to, Marta. It's safer like that. You know that Sam is working with the Resistance. When Ervin and I told him that you couldn't get into the Swedish embassy to obtain Schutz-Passes for your family, Sam found out that Mr. Wallenberg moves about to different locations to do his rescue work. We have an address. Come with us."

"Oh, Sam, how can we ever repay you?" I hugged him so tightly that he grunted in protest.

"You must bring photographs with you," he said.

I took out the family albums and flipped through the pages of smiling babies, solemn brides, and vacations by the lake, removing faded photographs that could substitute for passport pictures. It took a few minutes, but I finally had pictures of each of us. I wrapped them in a sheet of newspaper and carefully put them in my purse.

"Can Judit come with us?" I asked the boys.

"Not today. They're expecting only one person," Peter said.

"We'll have to ask them to put us up for the night, Marta," Sam said. "Peter can go home, but we can't risk it, especially if they give you Schutz-Passes. You don't want to be caught with six of them in your possession."

I wrote a quick note telling Mama that I wouldn't be

home until the next day. I asked her not to worry and promised to explain everything when I returned. I knew she would be furious with me and terrified, but it couldn't be helped.

After I grabbed my purse, we were on our way. I was careful to close our apartment door gently so I wouldn't wake Grandmama. In spite of the hot August sun, I covered the yellow star on my blouse with a sweater and prayed that we wouldn't be stopped by the Arrow Cross, the police, or the Germans.

"We're going to 2 Percel Street," Sam announced.

It took us a while to walk the long streets of apartment blocks. We were afraid to take the streetcar. Number 2 was a large and elegant building. We climbed to the third floor and rang the doorbell of a corner apartment. The door was opened a crack by a slight young man with the bluest eyes I had ever seen. He was dressed in a dark suit and had a brown rucksack in his hand. I was surprised by the sturdy hiking shoes on his feet.

"Can I help you?" he asked. He spoke Hungarian with a strong foreign accent.

Sam whispered something in his ear.

"Just a minute," the man said. He went back into the apartment, closing the door behind him. We waited silently on the doorstep until he reappeared a few minutes later.

"You must speak to Goldberg," he said. "He will help you." He noticed that I was staring at his hiking shoes. "A person never knows when he will have to march long distances," he said with a wry smile. "Good shoes can mean the difference between life and death."

He opened the door wider and motioned for us to go in. Then, with a wave of his hand, he headed down the stairs.

We found ourselves in a large apartment. The vast room was full of desks, the same kind that we used to have at school. There were at least a hundred little children sleeping on the desktops. A very fat man was standing in a corner of the spacious room, holding a crying child in his arms. The little boy couldn't have been more than four years of age. When the man saw us, he murmured to the little boy and gently put him down on an empty desk. The child fell asleep immediately.

"I am Goldberg," the man said. His Hungarian was very poor. "We speak quiet . . . little ones sleep." His smile was kind.

We introduced ourselves. Mr. Goldberg seemed to understand what we were saying to him.

"You meet Wallenberg. He let you in," he said.

"Wallenberg?" Peter asked. "A man opened the door for us, but he didn't tell us his name. He told us to speak to you."

"Man . . . Wallenberg, ya! He tell me you here. He say I listen. Why you here?"

I unbuttoned my sweater. The six-pointed star was bright against the white material of my blouse. Goldberg's face became solemn. I explained to him that we desperately needed Schutz-Passes.

"Please, sir," I pleaded. "We're hungry, we're afraid, but we want to live. We want to buy time until the war ends. The Schutz-Passes will do that for us. Please, sir, help us."

Goldberg sighed deeply. "You Swedish?" he asked. "Papa Swedish? Mama Swedish, eh?"

"None of us. We're Hungarians, but we're Jewish."

"I understand."

I repeated what Grandmama had told us. "My grandfather used to import lumber from Sweden."

"Lumber? Don't understand," Goldberg said.

"Trees, wood . . . Bring from Sweden," I explained.

"Trees! Trees! Good!" he cried. "When bring trees?"

"I don't know. Before I was born."

"Sweden trees, sure?"

I nodded. He looked at me for a long moment, scratching his chin pensively.

"Good, lumber good," he said. "Come."

He led us to a black roll-top desk below a tall window. With a key from his pocket he opened it, revealing several stacks of neatly piled documents.

"How many family?" he asked.

"Six of us, sir: my mother, brother, grandmother, aunt, cousin, and me."

"Have pictures?"

I handed the photos to him.

He deliberately counted out six official-looking documents from one of the stacks of papers in the desk.

"Passport, Schutz-Pass," he said, pointing to the documents.

He pulled down the roll-top, locked the desk, and the four of us went into the kitchen and settled at an old wooden table. Each of the documents in front of Goldberg had the word "Schutz-Pass" printed at the top. Each bore a replica of the Swedish crown and the signature of Minister Ivan Danielsson. All six protective passports were stamped by an official seal. I wrote out our names for Goldberg. He copied each one into a Schutz-Pass. He also filled in the date and pasted the photographs into the passports. He gave me all six protective passports, and I put them carefully into my purse.

"Thank you, sir! Thank you! You gave us life!" In my joy, I kissed his hand.

"No, no," he cried. "You thank Wallenberg, not me! I work here. Wallenberg, he bring Schutz-Pass here!"

"God bless you, sir, and God bless Mr. Wallenberg!"

Goldberg patted my hand. He pointed to the star on my blouse. "Take off. Not need . . . Schutz-Pass." He walked over to one of the kitchen cabinets and took out a large pair of scissors. "Take off," he said again.

I carried the scissors into the bathroom, took off my blouse, and unpicked the stitches. Then I cut the canary yellow material into tiny pieces and flushed them down the toilet. I gazed at myself in the mirror above the sink. The star was gone and the old Marta had reappeared. I felt light, as if I could fly.

Sam explained to Mr. Goldberg that it was dangerous for the two of us to return home that night because of the curfew. We said goodbye to Peter and he left. Goldberg gave us slices of black bread to munch on for supper, then we settled down for the night on the floor under the kitchen table.

Mama was waiting at the window when I returned home the next day. First she hugged me, then she started yelling at me.

"Thank God you're all right! How could you do this to me, Marta? You must have known I'd be frantic. And you're not wearing your star!"

"I'm sorry, Mama, but I had no choice." I stopped her torrent of words by taking her Schutz-Pass out of my purse and giving it to her. I handed around the others as well. Mama and Aunt Miriam wept. Ervin and Gabor whooped for joy.

"So honorable, good men *do* still exist in our world," Grandmama said.

"How did you get these Schutz-Passes?" Ervin asked. His voice was laced with envy.

I told them all about Sam's visit, and how we had gone to a safe house and met Goldberg and Wallenberg.

"Thank God your grandfather had business dealings with Sweden," Mama said.

The relief left us exhausted. The others slept, but I let myself out and knocked on Judit's door. I showed her and her mother my Schutz-Pass.

"Let me take you there. They'll help you. They were so kind."

"It's useless for Judit to go," Mrs. Grof said. "Our family never had any connection with Sweden."

"Please, Mother, let me go with Marta," Judit cried. "Perhaps they'll be able to do something for us anyway. Marta doesn't even have to wear a yellow star any more."

"We could tell them that our grandfathers were business partners, that both of them imported lumber from Sweden," I suggested.

"I don't think that's a good idea," Mrs. Grof said. "They'll probably check what you tell them. Then we might be in worse trouble than before."

No matter how hard Judit and I tried, we could not change her mother's mind.

· 7 ·

Denounced

Judit and I were standing in front of Aunt Miriam's dresser mirror, posing. I swept my hair up on top of my head.

"Do you think I look like Judy Garland?"

"No, actually, you look like me, Judit Grof!" She laughed.

It was true. Both of us had dark eyes and olive skin. We wore our shoulder-length brown hair in a pageboy like the actresses in American films. Judit's hair was naturally wavy, so this style was easy for her to achieve. I, on the other hand, had to tie my poker-straight locks in rags every night before going to bed to get the same effect. Judit was also a head taller than I was. Secretly, I envied her more womanly figure, although I never would have admitted it. My own chest still resembled a washboard.

"Do you girls ever stop talking? We're trying to concentrate," said Ervin. The boys were playing checkers on the floor. "We've been here for three months, and you two haven't run out of things to say. Come and play with us."

We sat down on the floor.

"Who's winning? Gabor again?" I asked.

"No," said Ervin.

"What's the matter with you?" I asked Gabor sarcastically. "Have you forgotten how to play?"

"Is something bothering you?" Judit asked.

"Oh, nothing. I just . . . Never mind," Gabor stammered. I was immediately sorry for having made fun of him.

"Are you crying?" Judit's brother, Adam, asked. He took advantage by skipping his red checker piece over Gabor's black one. "Beat ya!" he crowed.

"Quiet!" Ervin snapped, jabbing Adam in the ribs with his elbow. He turned to Gabor. "What's the matter?"

Gabor gave him a grateful look. My brother nodded back encouragingly.

Gabor cleared his throat. "Does anybody know the date today?" he asked in a reedy voice.

"August 19, 1944," Adam crowed. He liked to show off.

"I am supposed to have my bar mitzvah exactly one week from today. But with Father gone and the synagogue closed . . . Mother says my turn will come after Father comes home. I know she's right, but . . ." He stopped for a moment. "I'm so disappointed. I've been looking forward to reading from the Torah for so long, and who knows when Father will come home . . . if he ever does." His voice trailed off miserably.

"Don't even think of something so awful!" Judit said fiercely. "Your father will be home soon. You must believe that with all your heart!"

Gabor shook his head in resignation. "I hope so. I know God will help us. It's just that I was looking forward to my bar mitzvah so much."

I remembered how happy Ervin was at his own bar mitzvah the year before. Papa was so proud. And Gabor's family was more observant than mine.

"Why don't you explain your Torah reading to us?" I suggested. "And after Uncle Laci comes home, we can all go to the synagogue and see you get called up."

"Do you know your Torah portion?" Ervin asked.

"By heart. I've been practicing it for a couple of years."

"I like Marta's suggestion," Ervin said. "You can explain the meaning of your Torah portion on the same day that you were supposed to be having your bar mitzvah. Afterward, the four of us can have a little party in your honor. A party just for kids."

Each of us had found gifts to give Gabor to commemorate his bar mitzvah. Judit and Adam's present was a deck of cards – Gabor loved all kinds of games. I gave him my copy of *The Boys of Pal Street*. The novel was dog-eared because I'd read it over and over again. But his mouth really fell open when Ervin presented him with his pocket knife. Grandpa and Gran had given it to him for his own bar mitzvah, and he never went anywhere without it.

"I can't take this. It wouldn't be right," Gabor said. I could see by his expression that he wanted to keep the knife badly.

"I want you to have it," Ervin replied, awkwardly patting him on the shoulder.

"Thank you, Ervin. Thank you all," he said. He was beaming from ear to ear.

Gabor had a collection of American jazz records, so we pushed all the furniture except the sofa to the wall, piling the chairs and small tables on top of each other to give us more room. After we'd rolled up the Persian carpet that covered the parquet floor, there was a little space to dance. We turned up the music so loud that we didn't even hear Peter when he came in.

"Peter! You came at the right time," I said.

"I came to say goodbye. My parents are making me go to Pecs. Away from 'bad influences,' they say."

"*I'm* the bad influence?"

"You're the least of their worries now. They want to know why I won't enlist. By the way, you forgot to lock the door, you know. What's going on here?" He looked around and saw the records and the cake Grandmama had somehow managed to bake for us. "Are you having a party?"

Ervin stopped the music.

"Well, sort of," I said.

"I'm going to talk," said Gabor. "But first I'll lock the door."

Peter watched as Ervin and Gabor put satin yarmulkes on their heads. Gabor wrapped his father's tallis, his prayer shawl, around his shoulders, and Ervin wore Papa's. Judit, Adam, Peter, and I sat down on the sofa. Peter was beside me, holding my hand. All I could think of was that I might never see him again.

Gabor stood very straight, facing us. "My Torah portion is full of beautiful ideas," he said in a serious voice. "It discusses the sacredness of each individual human life. It also talks about how people should behave if the corpse of a murder victim is found in their community and how —"

A sudden banging shook the apartment door. My first thought was that whoever it was mustn't discover Peter. He looked around the room in a panic.

"Peter, get in the closet!" Ervin said. "Hurry up!"

Ervin and Peter rushed to a large mahogany wardrobe in the corner of the room and opened its double doors wide. Peter squeezed in behind Aunt Miriam's dresses. Ervin locked the wardrobe's door and put the key into his pocket.

The banging outside intensified. I shook my head to clear it. "Put the key back. They might notice it's missing," I told Ervin.

"You're right." Ervin pushed the large, old-fashioned metal key back into the lock on the wardrobe door. The banging grew still louder. The boys shoved their yarmulkes and the tallisim under the sofa cushions. The banging was becoming so loud that I feared the door would break down. We looked at each other anxiously.

"I'll do the talking," Ervin said. "Marta, let them in."

I took a deep breath and opened the door. Two policemen and a civilian with a pockmarked face pushed their way into the apartment. The handles of the policemen's revolvers were sticking out of the holsters on their hips. Their knee-high boots gleamed brightly, even under the dim electric lights.

"You took your sweet time answering the door, Jew," the older policeman snarled.

"I'm sorry, but we were listening to the phonograph and didn't hear you knocking," Ervin said. His tone was conciliatory. "What can we do for you, officer?"

"Mr. Szilard here," the older policeman said, pointing to the man with the pockmarked face, "reported to us that somebody from this apartment has been signaling the Americans."

It was only then that I recognized the pockmarked man as the janitor of the apartment house across the street.

"That's not true, officer!" Ervin cried. "We're loyal Hungarians. We wouldn't support the enemy."

"The Jew is lying!" yelled Szilard. The veins in his forehead bulged in an alarming manner. "I saw with my own two eyes these Jews sending light signals to the Americans. They were signaling them from their front window, across the street from us. They must be spies!"

Ervin gave the rest of us a warning look. Judit and Adam were holding hands for comfort, while Gabor glared at Szilard, his eyes full of hate. My own heart was racing so rapidly that I had trouble catching my breath.

"Take us to the room Mr. Szilard is talking about," the younger policeman ordered brusquely.

We led the three men to Aunt Miriam's bedroom, the only room in the apartment that faced the street. The curtains over the windows were kept wide open to let in the evening summer breezes. We closed the blackout curtains only when we had to turn on the lights.

The older officer switched on the lights but left the drapes open. The crystal chandelier cast gloomy shadows into the recesses of the room. My stomach somersaulted when I remembered that my aunt had hidden a radio under her bed. We listened to the Hungarian-language broadcasts of the BBC every evening. But fortunately, although the policemen looked around the room carefully, examining every nook and cranny, they did not bother to get down on their hands and knees to look under the bed. Nor did they seem inclined to search the rest of the apartment.

"Nothing here," the younger policeman announced, scratching his head.

The janitor was becoming more agitated by the moment. "The Jew is lying! Who are you going to believe – me or a dirty Jew?"

"You, of course, Mr. Szilard," the older policeman said reassuringly. "The Jews must have hidden their transmitter somewhere else. We'll take them down to headquarters. They'll tell the truth there soon enough." He turned off the lights, ready to leave the room.

I knew he was talking about torture. And Peter, hiding in the locked wardrobe – it was only a question of time before he was found. The moment seemed to last forever. I forced myself to look away from the policemen so I could think more clearly, more calmly. My eyes fell on the key cabinet hanging on the wall. This large cupboard filled with various household keys was attached to the back wall, right across from the open windows. The front panels of the ebony cabinet were decorated with silver inlays in the shape of peacocks. I had loved to trace the outlines of these birds with my fingers when I was a little girl. I noticed then that the peacocks' plumage gleamed brighter whenever the moonbeams peeked out from behind the clouds. I realized what must have happened. The janitor had mistaken the moonlight reflected by the silver peacocks for light signals being sent to the Americans.

"Look, sir," I said to the policemen. "The silver of the peacocks on the cabinet reflects the moonbeams. It's moonlight, not light signals, that Mr. Szilard saw."

The younger officer seemed to be convinced, but his older colleague looked doubtful. Somehow, I had to make him believe me.

"Let me prove to you, sir, exactly what did happen," I said to the older policeman earnestly. "Why don't you go over to Mr. Szilard's apartment, to the window that faces our house, and see for yourself whether I am telling you the truth? You'll see that as soon as the moon comes out from behind the clouds the silver inlay on the key cabinet reflects the light. While you're gone, we'll go into the parlor. That way, you'll know that we didn't touch a thing in here."

I turned to the younger policeman. "Why don't you stay with us to make sure that we don't leave the parlor?" I smiled at the officer pleasantly. I didn't want to give the impression that I was issuing orders.

After much deliberation, the skeptical older policeman and the janitor agreed to go across the street. They insisted that Ervin go with them. The rest of us filed in to the parlor. The young policeman threw himself down on the sofa, right on top of the boys' yarmulkes and tallisim. He pulled a rolled-up newspaper from the inside pocket of his uniform and began to read the sports page. We sat in silence, waiting, afraid to speak to one another.

The minutes dragged by. I tried to estimate how long Ervin and the two men had been gone – at least fifteen minutes. I became more and more worried with every passing second. Was there still enough air in the wardrobe for Peter to breathe? Just then, I heard a slight rustle from that direction. I stood up from my chair.

"Where are you going?" the policeman snapped.

"Just stretching my legs, sir," I answered. "Judit, why don't you offer the officer a slice of cake?"

Judit stared at me as if I had lost my mind. We were looking forward to eating every morsel ourselves.

"Give the officer some cake, Judit," I repeated. I walked to the table and pulled up another chair next to it. The back of the chair faced the room and the wardrobe.

Judit looked confused, but she did as I asked. She cut a slice of the cake, put it on a plate, then offered it to the policeman. The officer sat down at the table. His back was to the room and also to the wardrobe. While he concentrated on wolfing down the cake, I inched backwards, closer and closer to the wardrobe. Finally, keeping a large smile pasted on my face, I reached behind me and gently turned the key in the lock. Then I reached behind me again and pulled on the key, being careful not to dislodge it. The wardrobe door opened a crack. I coughed once again to cover the noise, but the officer was too busy eating to notice. I remained in front of the wardrobe, my hands on my hips, my legs slightly apart, as if I was waiting for Ervin and the two men to come back.

The seconds seemed to crawl by, but it couldn't have been more than another ten minutes before Ervin and the two men returned. The younger policeman was just finishing off his second helping of cake. Ervin rolled his eyes heavenward behind the policeman's back. Szilard, the janitor, had a sheepish expression on his face.

"Well, it seems that the girl was right this time," the older policeman said. "Whenever the clouds moved away from the moon, we could see the silver on the cabinet reflecting the light." He shook his forefinger at us threateningly. "Watch your step! You were lucky this time, but we'll be keeping an eye on you."

And with that, the policemen and the janitor were gone as abruptly as they had come. I rushed to the wardrobe and helped Peter climb out.

"I'm sorry for the noise," he said, "but my legs were cramping so badly I had to move them."

I was so overwhelmed by joy and relief that I couldn't even answer him. I just laid my head on his shoulder and laughed and cried at the same time.

Before he left for home, Peter offered to take the boys' tallisim with him.

"I'll keep them safe for you until the end of the war," he said. "It was a lucky thing you had the presence of mind to shove them out of sight under the sofa cushions or the policemen would have taken them."

Ervin and Gabor gratefully accepted Peter's offer. They lovingly folded Papa and Uncle Laci's prayer shawls and wrapped them up in a large sheet of newspaper. Nobody would have guessed what the square package in Peter's hand contained when he took it out of our apartment.

.8.

The New Year

On the last day of August, Mama left for work as usual. She was back an hour later.

"I've been fired," she announced. She sat rigid on a kitchen chair.

"What will we do?" asked Grandmama.

"Don't worry, dear. We have some jewelry to sell."

Grandmama went back to bed, so she did not hear Mama's weeping.

September came. As Rosh Hashanah, the Jewish New Year, approached, the days became cooler and the leaves yellowed on the trees. But there would be no prayers in the synagogues – they were all closed, and many had been defaced or burned to the ground. Nor was there food for a holiday meal – life was desperate in every Jewish family, not just ours.

To survive, we had traded away Mama's pearl necklace and Aunt Miriam's dainty bracelet with its Eiffel Tower charm and tiny bells – the pearl necklace brought us two dozen eggs and a bag of flour; the gold bracelet gave us two loaves of bread and a block of cheese.

I was in the kitchen helping Grandmama prepare something out of nothing for dinner. She was at the table transferring flour from a canister into a large bowl. She worked slowly, careful not to spill any. I sat at the table, kicking the leg.

"Don't shake the table, Marta," she said.

"What's for dinner?"

"We're eating your mama's pearl necklace today," she said wryly. She poured water from a pitcher into the flour and mixed the moist dough with a wooden spoon. "I am making *nokedli*," she said. "Come, watch me do it. Unfortunately, I already used up our eggs, so I can't put any into it."

She transferred the dough to a wooden bread board and cut it into water boiling in a cast-iron pot on the old-fashioned wood-burning stove. We had broken up our dining-room chairs for fuel. The dumplings quickly rose to the surface of the water.

"Who bought Mama's pearls?" I asked.

"Marika Marton, who else? How badly she wanted them! Even so, she took terrible advantage of your mother."

The door opened and Mama came into the kitchen,

catching the tail end of our conversation. "Who took advantage of me?" she asked.

"We're talking about Marika. Marta wanted to know who had bought your pearls."

"I wish you hadn't had to sell them, Mama." I always liked the way the pearls glistened against her throat; they made her neck seem so long and elegant.

"Papa will buy me another strand after the war," Mama said. "Nowadays, a loaf of bread is more precious than the rarest pearl." She walked over to the icebox and took out a small block of cheese. "Well, this is the end of Miriam's charm bracelet," she said, laughing. "I'll ask Marika if she has any friends who want to buy a ring." She held up her hand and examined the large gold signet ring on her middle finger. It was a gift from my father for their first wedding anniversary. The ring bore both their initials intertwined. "This should be good for a few loaves of bread."

"I won't hear of it, Nelly," Grandmama said. "You've sacrificed enough. I'll sell my necklace." Her fingers fondled the gold Star of David under her collar.

"I can't let you do that, Grandmama. Besides, I'm afraid there isn't much of a market for such things these days. It would be melted down for the gold. Aron can always buy me another ring, but your necklace is irreplaceable."

Grandmama nodded. "I'll wait, but only because Aron would want me to. You do realize, my dear, that we're only postponing the inevitable." She turned to me and looked me over, head to toe. "The child is skin and bones. She must eat. So must the others."

Mama did not reply. She grated the cheese into a small bowl. Grandmama drained the *nokedli* and melted the cheese in a frying pan on the stove.

"Marta," she said, "call the others, please. Dinner is ready."

Judit and I were lounging on my mattress. For once, we had some privacy. The adults were in the kitchen, and the boys were so noisy in the parlor that we could hear them through the closed doors.

"Do you realize that Rosh Hashanah is only three days away?" I asked my friend.

"Of course," she said. "I wish everything could be the way it was before the war. I used to love getting ready: my new shoes, a new dress. We used to go to my uncle Natan's for dinner."

"Well, things *aren't* the same. But I've been thinking: we can't go to synagogue, but we can still organize a holiday meal."

"How? We don't have money, and the grocer's shelves are always bare." Her stomach grumbled so loudly that I could hear it. "I'm so hungry," she said, embarrassed.

"Me too. I remember I used to eat so much on holidays that I felt I'd burst if I took another bite."

"Wouldn't it be wonderful to feel like that again?" Judit said. Her stomach growled even louder.

"What did you eat today?"

"Bean soup," Judit said. "Bean soup every day this week. Yuk! It gives me gas."

I held my nose. Judit stuck out her tongue.

"We've been eating *nokedli*," I told her. "Mama was able to buy flour and cheese. I love Grandmama's dumplings, but I don't want to eat them ever again."

Judit nodded. "I know how you feel. After the war ends, I'll never have beans. Not even once," she vowed.

"It doesn't seem right not to have a holiday meal to welcome in the New Year. Let's plan a special dinner like we used to have before the war. We'll get the groceries we need for it somehow."

"You're dreaming, Marta," Judit said. "There's nothing we can do. We were able to buy only a handful of beans, and you have only a little bit of flour."

"That's it! We have only one kind of food and you have only one kind of food. If we pool them, we can make something special. Let's speak to Mrs. Krausz on the fourth floor, the Kaufmanns on the fifth, and the Lazars next door to you. They might be interested in sharing as well."

"You're a genius, Marta. We won't have meat, but it will sure be better than plain old beans."

"Or plain old dumplings. Let's go to the grocer's tomorrow to see what else we can get," I suggested.

We went to the kitchen to talk to my family.

"I don't know . . . Cooking for four or five families – that's a lot of work, even if we are making only one dish," Mama said.

"Neither your mother nor I is a good cook," Aunt Miriam added.

"But I am! I think the girls' idea is absolutely wonderful!" Grandmama exclaimed. "It will actually be less work than usual. Each family can cook one dish and share it."

"Well, Grandmama, if you're quite sure that you're up to it. Promise you'll stop if it tires you. Remember your heart." Mama was worried.

Grandmama laughed. "Nothing is wrong with me. I'm fine. Why, I'm doing well even without my medication!" My grandmother's heart pills were no longer available at the pharmacy. "Come on, girls! We don't have much time to organize such a special meal."

The next morning, Judit and I visited neighbors in our apartment block to arrange for food and supplies. Mrs. Krausz volunteered to fry potato pancakes for all of us. She also sent two potatoes home to Grandmama. Mrs. Kaufmann on the fifth floor offered to make enough of her famous cucumber salad for everybody. The grocer had promised her fresh cucumbers, and she even gave us a package of yeast and butter so that Grandmama could bake a chala. The last family we spoke to, the Lazars, not only offered to cook rice, but were also able to spare a few spoonfuls of precious sugar.

"Aren't you girls clever!" Grandmama said when we showed off our booty.

First we wrote down what each family had promised to cook for our Rosh Hashanah menu, then we set out for the grocer's. We wanted to see what he had before we decided what we'd make for the meal.

"Good day, Mr. Kertesz," I said to the grocer behind the counter. I braced myself for his usual gruff "What do you want?" but it didn't come.

Instead, we got: "What can I do for you, my dears?"

"We have an important holiday coming up. We'd like to buy some food for it," Judit said.

My heart fell as I looked around the store. The shelves were almost completely bare. "I guess we came too late."

"No, no, my dear," the grocer said. He leaned forward and rubbed his palms together. The skin of his hands was ingrained with dirt. "I've been saving something for special customers. Two pretty girls like you certainly qualify." He reached under the counter and pulled out a burlap bag. "I have some lovely peas for you. How much do you need?"

"At least three kilograms," Judit said.

"How much will that cost?" I held my breath. Judit and I had only two hundred pengos between us. I was certain he would want at least six hundred.

"How much money do you have?" Kertesz asked.

"Only two hundred pengos," I told him.

"How fortunate!" he cried. "Three kilograms of peas will cost you exactly two hundred pengos." He measured the peas into the shopping bag I had brought with me from home.

"The peas look a little dry," Judit said.

"It's a little late in the season, but they're very fresh," the grocer answered.

"What luck," Judit whispered to me. "We'll have enough peas for everybody."

"Thank you, Mr. Kertesz, for letting us have the peas. You're a kind man."

An odd expression flickered across his face. It was gone so quickly, however, that I thought I must have imagined it.

"I'm glad to help. I know these are hard times for you," he said.

Judit and I had the kitchen to ourselves when we returned home. Grandmama was resting in her room and the boys were out. We took out two large metal bowls, one for the peas and one for the shells. I picked up a pod and squeezed it hard to open it. A few dry peas and two tiny bugs popped out and fell into the empty bowl with a hard ring. The bugs started climbing up the sides.

"Ugh!" Judit recoiled. My stomach lurched. I emptied the bowl into the kitchen sink and washed the bugs down the drain. Then I picked up another pod and squeezed it open. Once again, dry peas and black bugs in the bowl. The same thing happened over and over again with all the peas we shelled. It didn't matter whether the pod came from the top of the pile, the middle, or the bottom. All were infested with tiny black bugs.

"What are we going to do?" Judit wailed. "We spent all of our money on these disgusting peas. Do you think old Kertesz will give our money back?"

"There is no chance of that." I remembered the expression on the grocer's face when we thanked him for his kindness.

"What are we going to do?" Judit repeated. She sounded desperate.

I knew what we had to do, but the words did not come easily. "Kill the bugs and eat the peas."

Judit looked sick, and I felt the same.

"We have no choice," I continued. "If we don't cook these peas, none of us will have enough to eat. Everybody is counting on us for at least one good dish."

Judit nodded reluctantly. "If you're sure there's no other way."

"There isn't. Don't tell anybody about the bugs. It's bad enough that we know."

For the next hour, Judit and I took turns squeezing open pea pods. Using a wooden spoon, we fished out the tiny black bugs crawling around in the bowl. By the time

Grandmama returned to the kitchen, the bowl was filled with slightly dry but edible peas.

I was in the women's balcony in the synagogue on Dohany Street on the eve of Rosh Hashanah. I leaned over the railing and peered down at the men's section. Papa and Ervin, Uncle Laci and Gabor were standing side by side, their tallisim draped over their shoulders. They bent and bowed in prayer. Ervin looked up and nodded to me. I nodded back.

The cantor chanted: "Remember us unto life, O King Who desires life, and inscribe us in the Book of Life – for Your sake, O Living God."

I lost track of my surroundings, and my entire being focused on the words I was saying: "On Rosh Hashanah will be inscribed and on Yom Kippur will be sealed how many will pass from the earth and how many will be created; who will live and who will die; who will die at his predestined time and who before his time; . . . But repentance, prayer, and charity remove the evil of the decree!"

Papa and the others were so real that I had only to reach out to touch them. Then the moment was gone.

I tried to focus on the prayers I held in my hand, but the words in my prayer book blurred then faded away until the pages became completely blank. I searched and searched, but the prayers had disappeared. Suddenly, I was in a strange place where everything was shadowy and out of focus. A whirling black cloud surrounded me, and I couldn't find my way no matter how hard I tried.

Then I was with Papa and Uncle Laci in a deep forest, saying the same words of prayer. Grandpa and Gran were there too, but then all of them disappeared. A shiver ran down my spine.

I woke up. My heart was hammering, the hair at the nape of my neck was damp. The stillness was broken only by Grandmama's gentle snoring. Tears ran down my cheeks as I whispered to myself, Please, God! Please, God! Don't let them kill us! Let us survive! Let us live! I even made a special bargain with God: I'll be good! I'll be kind! I'll never, ever hurt anyone as long as you let us live, dear God!

On the eve of Rosh Hashanah, the Grofs joined us as we crowded around the kitchen table. Mrs. Krausz's potato pancakes were piled up beside a bowl of Mrs. Kaufmann's cucumber salad. Our peas were on their holiday tables.

Ervin and Gabor covered their heads with yarmulkes. Ervin blessed the chala Grandmama had baked. Water had to substitute for wine. The light from the two tall candles in the center of the table cast mysterious flickering shadows over our faces. Grandmama's dish of peas in sauce was the hit of the evening.

"You're a talented cook, Grandmama," Mrs. Grof exclaimed as she took another helping.

"I do my best," Grandmama said modestly, though I could sense how much the compliment pleased her. "The girls deserve all the credit."

"The peas are really delicious," said my mother. "Anybody for seconds?"

"I'll have some more," Gabor said.

Ervin and Adam just held out their plates to Mama.

"What about you girls? Don't you like peas? Neither of you took any. There is enough here for everybody," said Aunt Miriam. She reached for the ladle with one hand and my plate with the other.

I gripped my dish protectively. "No, thank you. I don't feel like eating peas today."

Judit was giggling and running the fingers of her left hand up and down her right forearm, imitating crawling insects. "I don't want any peas either," she announced.

"What's the matter with you two?" Aunt Miriam asked. "The peas are very tasty." She grabbed hold of Judit's plate and ladled a generous helping onto it.

I tried unsuccessfully to stifle a chortle.

"What's wrong?" Mrs. Grof asked sharply.

"Nothing," I mumbled.

Mama looked around the table. "Good food, good friends, laughter." Her face darkened. "If only . . ."

She didn't have to finish her sentence. If only Papa were

with us, if only her parents were safe, if only Uncle Laci would come home, if only Judit's father would return. If only they'd been with us, I wouldn't have cared about anything – not the war, not the hunger, not my disappointment over school.

Mama reached across the table and grasped my hand tightly. "Don't worry, love! The war will be over soon, and then Papa will be coming home." Her voice sounded hollow, as if she were trying to convince both of us at the same time.

"Yesterday, Sam Lazar from the apartment next to us told me that the Soviets and the Americans are getting much closer," Mrs. Grof said brightly.

"That's wonderful news," Mama said.

"Lazar also had some not-so-wonderful news," Mrs. Grof added in a more somber tone. "He said the Germans are becoming so panicky that they're speeding up their plans to deport all of us. Hundreds of empty cattle cars are waiting at the Keleti railway station to take us away before the Soviets or the Americans arrive."

A cold draft seemed to have entered the room. I couldn't have swallowed another morsel of food if my life had depended on it.

"Are you sure about this, Rachel?" Mama asked.

Mrs. Grof shrugged her shoulders. "I don't know. It's a rumor, but in these times . . ." As her voice trailed off, my heart filled with terror.

Gabor looked around the table at our worried faces. "We'll be all right," he said. "God will protect us."

Ervin's face turned red. "We have to protect ourselves, Gabor! Can't you see that? God has turned His face away from us! We have to rely on ourselves."

The boys glared at each other. I had never seen either one of them get even mildly upset with the other.

Finally, Ervin broke the silence. "Tomorrow Gabor and I will try to find out what's happening," he said in a milder tone.

"Be very careful!" Mama cried. "You know what can happen!"

"We have our Schutz-Passes," Ervin said. He sounded brave, but he was grasping the edge of the table so tightly that his knuckles were white.

"You don't want to test your Schutz-Pass if you don't have to," Mama warned. "The Germans and the Hungarian police, they're animals. What if they decide not to accept it?"

The warmth around the table had vanished completely. My teeth were chattering and the glowing candles were flickering out, along with my hopes for a happy future. What would the next days, the next weeks, and the next months hold for us? Would we be deported to the camps, never to return? I had never heard of anyone who was taken away and came home again – not Gran and Grandpa, not Ida, who wrote that nice postcard to us from the Waldsee.

142

And Papa . . . he had not written home for so long. The thought was too painful even to contemplate.

If I was gone, would Peter remember me? Probably, but for only a short time. I knew that I already had to concentrate really hard whenever I wanted to visualize Papa's face, and I loved Papa so much. Peter would remember what I looked like less and less every day. Well, at least I knew exactly what I had to do to prevent *that* from happening.

· 9 ·

Remembrance

Judit had often talked about her uncle Natan. Before the war, he had been one of the most famous photographers in all of Budapest. Judit's aunt had died when her youngest cousin was born, and Natan raised the baby and his two older sons by himself. Everybody in Judit's family considered Natan to be the luckiest of men – not only because he was the father of three wonderful sons, but also, oddly enough, because he walked with a pronounced limp, the result of a childhood bout of polio. His disability exempted Natan from being sent to a forced labor camp. His sons were not as fortunate, however; all three young men were digging ditches on the Russian front. Mrs. Grof had not had any news of her nephews for several months.

The day his sons waved their last goodbye from the back of an army truck, Natan tore off the yellow star that was on his shirt and moved all of his meager belongings to a basement apartment located below a photographer's studio on Kerepesi Road, far from the Jewish district. As soon as the studio's owner saw Natan's portfolio, he offered Judit's uncle a job. Judit had once shown me a photograph Natan had taken of her on her birthday the year before. The photograph, while not particularly glamorous, had captured my friend's quiet goodness, her sense of mischievous fun. The Judit in the picture was a real person. That's how I wanted Peter to remember me.

If the unthinkable happened, I didn't want to become a shadowy outline in Peter's memory. I wanted him to remember me the way I was and be reminded of who I might have been. I was certain that if Natan took a picture of me, Peter would never be able to forget me. He would remember our conversations in the little café, the glistening candles on the table at the Shabbos dinner he shared with my family, and most important, our stolen kiss in the ivy's embrace at the Casino. The day after the Jewish New Year, I set out for Uncle Natan's studio at 26 Kerepesi Road.

I told my family only that I was going for a long walk. Judit had given me careful directions, so I knew the way and was quite certain that I wouldn't get lost. I had no money for a streetcar ticket, so I walked and walked. When I passed the Keleti railway station, I crossed the street and fixed my eyes on the ground. Unfortunately, I looked up too soon. The long, long line of empty cattle cars parked on the steel rails leading into the station hypnotized me. I stood there staring at them for a long moment. The bulge of the Schutz-Pass in my pocket was comforting.

I couldn't help myself – I broke into a run even though I knew it was foolish. I kept running, terrified, barely aware where I was heading. I ran and ran and ran, my breath ragged. From the corner of my eye, I saw the tall white crosses of a Christian cemetery straining toward the sky.

The window of the photographer's studio at 26 Kerepesi Road was boarded up. A rusty padlock hung from the iron grille barring the entrance. I hurried down the worn stone steps leading to Natan's basement apartment. Stained green curtains covered the window and red paint flaked off the door. I banged on it. No response. I banged again, even harder. Where could Natan be? Judit had said that her uncle rarely left his apartment. I tried the door one last time, but the building remained silent. I was already at the top of the steps when a reedy voice stopped me.

"Who are you?"

"My name is Marta Weisz. Your niece Judit Grof is my best friend," I said to the small gnome standing in the doorway. The little man was so bald that the midday sun's rays reflected off the top of his head.

"I am Natan Donat," the man said, beckoning me to come down. "Come in," he added, standing aside.

We entered the tiny apartment. A blackened wood-burning stove in the corner had stained the walls of the room a dirty gray. The soles of my shoes stuck to the squalid linoleum. A rickety brown table and chair stood by a chipped porcelain sink on the left wall. Across from them was a brown settee whose springs had escaped the tweedy material in several places. Natan motioned for me to sit down. I lowered myself gingerly onto the sofa, careful to avoid the springs. Natan perched on the edge of the table.

"So, Judit's friend, what can I do for you?" he asked.

"I saw the photographs you took of Judit on her birthday, and I was hoping you could take one of me too," I explained. "I have no money to pay you, but I could do some work for you in return. Like cleaning your apartment."

Natan observed me for a moment. "So my apartment isn't clean enough for you?"

"No, no! I just –"

"Never mind!" He silenced me with a wave of his hand. "I don't take photographs any more. Why should I? What's worth preserving?" he asked. I had the feeling that he had forgotten he was addressing me, that he was really talking to himself. Suddenly, he looked at me as if he'd just remembered that I was there. "I don't have a camera," he said in a rough voice. "The Germans took it. I couldn't take your picture even if I wanted to." I could feel tears welling up in my eyes. "Why do you want to be photographed?" he asked abruptly.

"We heard that cattle cars have arrived at the Keleti station, that they are here to deport us. I have a friend, a boy . . ."

"Go on," Natan said.

"I want to give him my photograph. I don't want him to forget me when I'm gone."

"I see," Natan said. "You're quite right. The trains arrived three days ago. How old are you?"

"Fifteen."

"And the boy?"

"He is a year older than I am."

"The same age as my youngest boy," Natan said. "Exactly the same age as my son."

He stood for a long moment, his expression guarded. Then he crouched down and crawled under the wooden table. I inched toward the door. He took a penknife out of his pocket and used it to ease up the edge of the linoleum by the wall. A large square of the grimy floor covering rolled away, revealing a small wooden trap door. He pried the door open with his knife and retrieved a package wrapped in brown oil paper. He unwrapped a large black camera and several rolls of film.

"We're in business," he said, cackling.

After loading up his camera, Natan began to photograph me. He had me sitting on the couch, standing in the doorway, looking over my shoulder, smiling, laughing, and in one picture, thinking sad thoughts. Finally, he put his camera down.

"This should give me enough to work with. You have an interesting face. I would have liked to have taken more pictures of you, but I have to be careful with my film. I can't buy any more, and I have only the few rolls that I have hidden. Come back in a week and I'll have your photo ready."

"Thank you so much! I meant it about your apartment. When should I come to clean it?"

"Don't worry about it, Judit's friend. This rat's nest is beyond redemption. As you can see, a dirty floor has its uses," he said with the ghost of a smile. "Just come back to pick up your photo next week."

I thanked him and set out for home. It was a beautiful fall afternoon and the gentle autumn sun warmed my face. The trees along the boulevard were crowned in red and gold. But as I was passing the Christian cemetery on Kerepesi Road, an ominous buzzing sounded. I looked up at the sky. A large smoke rectangle signaled that the Americans were back. I was thrilled and terrified at the same time.

The first bomb hit the ground a few feet from me. The force of the explosion threw me backwards, against the stone wall surrounding the cemetery. The closest building was too far away to reach safely, so I ran into the cemetery to find shelter. Hundreds of graves with ornate headstones stood next to each other, row after neat row. I crouched down, cowering at the foot of a tall marble headstone in the shape of a cross, and covered my ears. The buzzing of the planes overhead intensified. Suddenly, a flash of fire, a deafening bang, and some kind of projectile flew with tremendous force out of a grave on my right. The object hit the ground right beside me. A grinning skull rolled up against my feet. A fragment of flying bone scraped my cheek. The planes kept on buzzing and buzzing and buzzing, as if a hive of monstrous bees was attacking the cemetery. Within seconds, all the graves were spilling their dreadful contents. The shower of bones blanketed the graves like unseasonable snow. Mindless of the danger, I jumped up and ran back to the street. My screams were lost in the roaring of the planes. Again, I ran and ran and ran. I ran as if the Devil himself was chasing me, with bombs landing to my left and to my right. A shower of leaflets released by the attacking airplanes fluttered to the ground, but I was too terrified to stop and pick one up. I just kept on running. Then suddenly, I realized that I could once again hear my own ragged breathing. The swarm in the sky had flown away.

I had calmed down by the time I neared home. Ervin was waiting for me on the street, a piece of paper clutched in his hand. He grabbed my arm and pulled me through the iron gates into the entryway.

"The Americans bombed the large Christian cemetery on Kerepesi Road, near the Keleti railway station," he cried.

"Then they dropped these leaflets all over the city, threatening to bomb every Christian cemetery in Budapest if the Jews are deported." Ervin shoved the paper into my hands but didn't give me a chance to read it. "I heard that the cattle cars are already pulling out of the station. And they're empty!" he shouted jubilantly. He grabbed both of my hands and started jumping up and down in his exuberance. Finally, he noticed my disheveled appearance. "What happened to you?"

I kept my voice cool. "Oh, nothing. I'm just dressed too warmly."

I gave the same excuse to the rest of my family. Only Judit knew the truth. A week later, I returned to Uncle Natan's studio to pick up my photograph. Twenty-six Kerepesi Road had become a large hill of rubble.

· 10 ·

Ten Long Days

J pulled up the collar of my coat against the chilly October air and hurried along with three precious potatoes for our evening meal. I was almost home when a military truck appeared in the road. A loudspeaker on the back blared over and over again: "My fellow citizens! This is Admiral Horthy speaking. Please turn on your radios."

I raced through the gates and up the stairs. Ervin had pulled Aunt Miriam's radio from its hiding place and was adjusting the dial to Hungarian State Radio. The regent's solemn voice filled the room. "The war is lost," he announced.

He explained that Hungary was withdrawing her support of Germany against the Soviet Union, that a cease-fire was in effect. It took us a stunned moment of silence to realize that we were no longer at war. We hugged and kissed and laughed and cried at the same time. Ervin grabbed Mama's hands and danced her around the room.

"I never thought I'd live to see this day," Grandmama said. "Aron will be coming home soon."

"Never forget today's date, children! October 15, 1944, is the day our lives were spared," Mama cried.

Pandemonium broke out. People rushed back and forth, banging on neighbors' doors with the wonderful news. I ran over to Judit's, but she had already heard. We went down to the street. Jewish people were pouring out of yellow-star houses. They ripped their stars off their garments and piled them up into a small mountain in the middle of the road. Somebody threw a lighted match and our mountain of shame turned into a bonfire.

"This can't be happening! It's just too wonderful to be true!" I cried over and over.

I was right. The moment of hope had been an illusion. The really bad times were just beginning.

Later, we learned that the Germans had forced the regent to sign over the powers of government to the Fascist Arrow Cross Party, led by Ferenc Szalasi. Szalasi and the Arrow Cross hated Jewish people with an all-consuming passion. I realized that the official policy of the new government was to destroy us. Our happy mood quickly gave way to a gnawing terror and an overwhelming sorrow. But we went to bed without giving voice to our fears. I tossed and turned for hours before sleep claimed me.

The next day, a new proclamation appeared on the lamppost in front of our block. Once again, Jews were ordered to wear yellow stars on their garments. Nobody was exempt, not even those of us who had been issued Schutz-Passes. Anybody caught disobeying this edict would be punished by death. We spent a tearful evening sewing stars on our clothes once again.

While we were getting ready for bed that night, Sam Stein appeared at our door. He was flushed and out of breath. Mama asked him to sit down.

"I can't. I'm trying to reach as many friends as I can. I still have a lot of people to contact," he said. "I came to warn you. Be careful! Now that they are in power, the Arrow Cross may not recognize your Schutz-Passes. If they cause you problems, send for Mr. Wallenberg. He'll deal with them."

Sam's advice had left me sleeping fitfully, and a few hours before dawn loud shouting and banging in the courtyard woke me. I sat up on my mattress, then crawled out of bed and almost tripped over my scuffed oxfords, neatly lined up on the floor. The parquet was cold beneath my feet, so I slipped on my shoes and tiptoed to the window to peek out into the courtyard

"Marta, what's happening? Is something wrong?" my grandmother asked. She was sitting up in her bed, wiping her eyes.

"I don't know. Something's going on outside."

I parted the curtains and looked out. The courtyard was dimly lit by a single lamppost. Several figures were moving about, but I couldn't see their faces in the semi-darkness. Then more people appeared. They were followed by a man in a uniform – no more than a boy really – who was pointing a gun at their heads. The young man's hair was burnished gold in the lamplight. He wore an Arrow Cross uniform, his high, shiny boots bright even in the semi-darkness. When they all stopped under the lamppost, I could finally see their features. His rifle was aimed at Judit and her mother.

There was a sudden loud banging on the front door of our apartment. We had by now all been awakened by the commotion and were gathered in the doorway of my room.

"Grandmama, what do you think? Should we open the door?" Mama asked urgently. "I don't know what to do."

"What choice do we have?" Grandmama said. "We have to let them in."

We went into the parlor. Aunt Miriam began to cry, silent tears flowing down her cheeks. Ervin and Gabor were heading to the front door when it splintered on its hinges under the weight of heavy boots. Two boys in Arrow Cross uniforms with drawn guns rushed in.

"Out! Out!" screamed the first one, waving his gun in Mama's face. "Come with us!"

"Why? What do you –" Ervin's voice was silenced by a vicious kick to his groin. He dropped to the floor, groaning.

Mama turned to help him. The gun barrel of the second Arrow Cross soldier stopped her.

"Out! Out!" he barked.

Gabor and I helped Ervin up. His face was ashen, but at least he was able to shuffle toward the door. We all followed him – except for Grandmama.

"Come on, old lady! Get going!"

"No!" she said quietly. "No, I won't!"

The Arrow Cross thug's hand moved so rapidly that I almost missed it. The heel of his rifle made a loud thud against my grandmother's temple, and she crumpled to the ground. The color ran out of her cheeks, out of her hands, even out of her knobby legs sticking out from her night-gown. A single thin rivulet of blood trickled down her still face. I knelt beside her and arranged her clothing to cover her legs modestly. Her gold Star of David necklace glistened against the whiteness of her nightdress. Once again, the movie of my imagination switched on. I was watching events unfolding around my celluloid self. The girl in the film smoothed down her grandmother's soft hair and closed her grandmother's staring eyes. Then suddenly, without any warning, the movie in my head began to fade. I tried to hold on to it desperately, but it became fainter and fainter until it disappeared.

Mama was bleating from grief.

"Get up, you old biddy!" screamed the Arrow Cross

youth, shoving the barrel of his gun into Grandmama's side. Even his friend seemed sickened.

"Stop it, Zoli! Stop it! Can't you see the old woman is dead?"

His friend leaned over Grandmama and put his pimply face close to her mouth and his grimy hand on her neck. His fingernails were blackened with dirt.

"Yeah, you're right! The old bitch is gone!" he snarled, kicking the still form again. "Ho! What have we here?" He leaned down and tore the shiny Star of David necklace from Grandmama's neck.

"What do you want that for?" exclaimed the second Arrow Cross youth. "It's Jew stuff!"

"It's gold!" the murderer protested. He scratched his head. "Yeah, you may be right!" He flung the necklace to the floor. It fell next to my feet.

"Come on! Come on! Hurry up!" yelled the second Arrow Cross youth, waving us out of the room. I crouched down on the pretext of tying my shoelaces and slipped the necklace into one of my brown oxfords. The sharp edges of the star pricked the sole of my foot even through my sock. I found the pain reassuring.

The courtyard was crowded by the time we got there. A dozen Arrow Cross youths with rifles were separating the men from the women. Ervin, Gabor, and Adam were forced at gunpoint to join a group of boys and old men standing on the far side of the courtyard. Mama, Aunt Miriam, and I were led by the guards to a group of Jewish women gathered on the opposite side. We huddled together, grieving, unable even to comfort each other. I kept seeing Grandmama's face and the trickle of red blood against her bleached complexion.

All of us were in our nightclothes. I was more fortunate than many of the others because I was wearing shoes. But even so, the cold of the October night made my teeth chatter. Judit sidled up to me.

"Where's your grandmother?"

"She is dead."

Judit asked no questions.

The Arrow Cross closed in on both groups. The one in charge planted himself in the middle of the courtyard and addressed us through a hand-held megaphone.

"Long live Szalasi! Heil Hitler!" he thundered, his arm stiffly extended into the air. He turned toward the men. "Jewish scum! You'll finally get what you deserve! You lazy good-for-nothings – you'll make yourselves useful to our beloved nation for the first time in your miserable lives!" he raved, spraying spittle into the night air like a snake spraying poison. "Take away these lazy Jewish dogs," he ordered. "Even the sight of them offends me!"

Within minutes, the Arrow Cross soldiers had lined up Ervin, Gabor, Adam, and the others and began marching them out of the courtyard at gunpoint. My own cries were drowned out by the wailing of the women around me. My aunt and I had to keep Mama from running after Ervin.

"Let go of me!" Mama cried, straining against our arms.

"Nelly, we can't. They'll kill you!" Aunt Miriam cried.

"They'll kill the boys too," said a weeping Mrs. Grof.

At that moment, elderly Mrs. Kaufmann from the fifth floor broke away from the crowd of women and ran toward her only child, Lali, who was standing at the rear of the group of men and boys. She was quickly halfway across the courtyard, her arms flung out in the direction of her son, beseeching the Arrow Cross guards to free her beloved child. A shot rang out. Mrs. Kaufmann fell to the ground with a high-pitched cry and lay motionless. Lali's screams pierced the deathly silence that suddenly enveloped us, but he was led out of the courtyard with the others.

When the boys were gone, the Arrow Cross official turned back to the group of weeping women.

"Now listen!" he thundered. We drew closer to each other. "Nobody, absolutely nobody, is to leave this block until further notice. Every entrance to your apartment house will be guarded by one of my men. They have orders to shoot if any of you tries to leave." He pointed a menacing finger at us.

The officer turned his back to us and began to shout orders at his soldiers. Several of them made lewd comments about the young girls and women standing unprotected in their nightgowns in front of them. I hugged myself to ward off their words, the bone-chilling cold, and the numbing sadness of my heart.

"Pretend they're not here!" Judit whispered fiercely, linking her arm through mine.

"I can't!"

Judit didn't answer – there was nothing to say. We watched in silence as the Arrow Cross murderers marched off, leaving behind armed guards at the two entrances to our block.

Mama, Aunt Miriam, and I helped to drag Mrs. Kaufmann's body into the building. By the time we returned to our apartment, an eternity seemed to have passed. We lifted the shattered front door and leaned it against the frame. As we went into the kitchen, we were careful to avert our eyes from the parlor's open door.

"What will we do? What will we do?" Aunt Miriam moaned.

My mother, dry-eyed, didn't answer her. "We must take care of Grandmama," she finally said. She got up from the table with a deep sigh.

First Mama and then Aunt Miriam said goodbye. I kissed Grandmama's icy hands and tried to memorize the texture of her skin, the softness of her cheeks. Together we straightened her lifeless limbs. We tidied her clothing and combed her hair tenderly. Grandmama had always been so proud of her thick and curly hair.

"We have no water to wash her with," Aunt Miriam said, weeping.

Mama was shaking like a leaf. "We have no shroud either, so we'll have to wrap her in a white sheet."

The only white sheet she could find was the one Grandmama had brought with her when we'd moved into the yellow-star house. She had appliquéd it for her trousseau before she had married my grandfather.

"She must not be left alone." Mama spoke quietly. "We'll take turns sitting with her and reciting the psalms."

"We have no prayer book," said Aunt Miriam. "I put it into Laci's knapsack when he was taken away."

"Perhaps one of your neighbors would have one," Mama suggested.

"I can't think of anybody. A prayer book is dangerous these days." Aunt Miriam's tears were turning to hysteria.

"Maybe you should take her to lie down, Mama. I'll stay with Grandmama first. I'll say Psalm 23 for her."

Mama looked at me gratefully and led Aunt Miriam to her bed, then I sat down on the floor beside my beloved grandmother and whispered my farewells to her for the last time. "Goodbye, my darling Grandmama, goodbye. I'll never forget you. I'll love you forever."

When I was finished, I began to recite the words Grand-mama had taught me:

> The Lord is my shepherd; I shall not want.
> He maketh me to lie down in green pastures:
> He leadeth me beside the still waters.
> He restoreth my soul:
> He leadeth me in the paths of righteousness for his
>   name's sake.
> Yea, though I walk through the valley of the shadow
>   of death, I will fear no evil:
> for thou art with me; thy rod and staff they comfort
>   me.
> Thou preparest a table before me in the presence of
>   mine enemies:
> thou annointest my head with oil; my cup runneth
>   over.
> Surely goodness and mercy shall follow me all the
>   days of my life:
> and I will dwell in the house of the Lord for ever.

I repeated the psalm until I was so hoarse that I could hardly form the words. Then I must have dozed off because a light tap on my shoulder startled me back to consciousness. It was Mama coming to relieve me.

"Go and get some sleep, darling," she said.

I returned to the room I had shared with my grand-mother. Sadness overwhelmed me when I saw her empty bed standing next to my mattress, but I was so exhausted that sleep claimed me as soon as my head hit my pillow.

When I awoke a few hours later, I thought for the first time about the necklace I had hidden in my shoe. So many terrible things had happened over the past few hours that I had forgotten all about it. Where to put it? I looked around the room, but no hiding place called out to me. The necklace was too precious to let out of my sight. I liked the idea of having it with me all the time, so I lifted up the insole of my oxford and carefully put the necklace into the very bottom of my shoe. Then I smoothed the insole over the necklace and patted it down. Only the faintest outline of the six-pointed star was visible. I was certain that once I'd worn my shoe a few times, even this faint mark would disappear.

Our food ran out after the second day of our imprisonment. I was so hungry that even the murky liquid in which we had boiled noodles tasted delicious when I greedily slurped it down. But soon it was gone too. By the fourth day, I wondered how much longer it would be before gnawing hunger would claim us and we too would be lying with the dead in the cool cellar of the building. The cellar had become a make-shift morgue for a toddler and a grandfather, the Lazars' pretty young daughter, Grandmama, and Mrs. Kaufmann. Every day someone we knew was carried down the dark steps.

We became weaker and weaker. Sores had formed inside my mouth, and my lips were cracked and bleeding. We spent most of the day sleeping in a semi-stupor. On the fifth day, as I was dozing listlessly, loud knocking woke me. I tried to stand up, but the room whirled around me. The next thing I knew, someone was supporting my head and forcing a spoonful of potato soup down my throat. I opened my eyes and found myself looking into Madam's stern face.

"Welcome back, Marta," she said in her usual formal manner. She allowed her lips to relax into a smile.

"Madam, what are you doing here? Who let you in? And Mama and my aunt . . ."

"One step at a time, Marta. Let me explain. When I heard that the yellow-star houses had been sealed, I knew your family must be hungry. I've tried to get in to see you every single day, but the guards at the gate wouldn't take a bribe. Thank goodness new guards were posted this morning. They turned out to be much more co-operative."

Madam fed me soup as she talked. Soon the room stopped spinning and I began to feel like myself again. I spooned soup into Mama's mouth, then she fed Aunt Miriam. Madam had also brought a block of cheese with her and a loaf of dark rye bread. We shared them with Judit and her mother.

Every single day for the next five days, Madam smuggled in some kind of food – a loaf of bread, potatoes, and beans to make soup. We were still hungry, but at least we were alive. On the tenth day of our captivity, however, a dozen Arrow Cross soldiers stormed our building. Once again, everything changed for the worse.

· 11 ·

Mr. Wallenberg

This time when we lined up in the courtyard, there were fewer of us. The faces around me were more haggard and much thinner than before. We had remembered the bone-chilling cold from the last time the Arrow Cross had descended upon us, so now everybody had put on winter clothing even though it was four o'clock in the morning and we'd been given only a few minutes to get dressed. I also remembered to put my Schutz-Pass in my pocket. Judit had even thrown a winter blanket over her coat for extra warmth, but in her haste, she had forgotten to pull on her shoes. She hopped up and down in one spot to keep her feet from freezing in the flimsy bedroom slippers she was wearing.

The younger women and children were quickly separated from the rest of the group and marched out of the courtyard at gunpoint. There were no goodbyes. The Arrow Cross guards prodded us with the muzzles of their guns while Judit and I clung together in a futile attempt at protection. Despite the men's threats, our progress was slow. If anyone stopped or even paused, a deafening shot rang out. We learned to step over the bodies and keep moving. We had no choice. The streets were littered with hundreds of corpses whose faces were covered with sheets of newspaper. I wondered if I knew any of the victims. Could Ervin and Gabor and Adam be among those lying on the ground? I looked and looked with morbid curiosity. I couldn't help myself.

The long march continued. At least a hundred more young women and children joined us at different points. The rays of the rising sun escaped the glowering clouds like punctuation marks, emphasizing the desperation on our faces. We finally stopped at the foot of the Chain Bridge, spanning the Danube River. By then, choking fear had gripped my hands, my belly, and my feet. Several people on their way to work had gathered around our group, chatting, laughing, pointing fingers in our direction. One fat old woman in a black babushka broke away from the crowd and walked up to Judit. Without looking into her face or acknowledging her existence with a glance or a word, she grabbed the blanket off Judit's shoulders, turned on her heels, and walked away with it. Judit stood staring after her with an open mouth. I squeezed her arm.

"Don't say anything! Pretend nothing happened"

"But I . . ."

Her voice trailed off as two of the Arrow Cross brutes dragged a young mother and her twin sons to the front of the crowd. One of the little boys was crying and the other sucked his thumb. Both were clinging to their mother, who tried to shield them with her arms. The guards tied a thick rope around the waist of each of the little boys, then wound it around the waist of their protesting mother. They next bound the mother's feet with a heavy metal chain. Using the barrels of their guns, they shoved the pathetic trio to the very edge of the Danube. Three of the Arrow Cross guards then lined up in a straight line and pointed their guns at the distraught mother and the frightened children. She covered her boys' eyes with her hands just before a loud shot rang out. Blood spurted out of the mother's mouth as she catapulted into the murky river, dragging her screeching little sons after her. The bubbles on the turgid waters were soon erased by angry waves. A gray seagull looked on for a moment, then lost interest, flapped its dirty wings, and was gone. Everything was so quiet that the sudden collective intake of breath of the Jewish captives could clearly be heard. Suddenly, the loud clapping of the onlookers broke the silence. The skies wept in sympathy.

We marched at gunpoint in the pelting rain for hours. We were soaked to the skin, and Judit's plaid bedroom slippers were in tatters. Finally, we arrived at a cavernous brick factory on the Buda side of the river. Our guards led us into a dark warehouse used to dry bricks. The huge space was dimly lit by a few grimy windows near the ceiling. I tried to get my bearings, but it was too dark to see. Slowly, I was able to make out what seemed to be hundreds and hundreds of bodies lying on the floor or leaning against the walls. Suddenly, I tripped and fell. My leg was caught in a deep hole. Judit yanked me out with all her might. As my eyes became accustomed to the semi-darkness, I saw that the entire floor was dotted with air vents like the one I had stepped into. Those who lost their footing in these holes were in danger of being trampled by the surging crowd.

We pushed our way to a corner of the vast room. Brick dust covered the walls and even the ceiling. It stuck to our clothes, giving us a ghostly appearance, made our eyes sting, and got into our noses and our mouths, making it hard to breathe.

"I feel as if I'm under water, as if I'm choking," Judit said.

"Me too! I'm afraid I'll throw up."

My stomach grumbled, but there was no water or food. When anyone asked to go to the washroom, a rifle butt or a kick by a polished boot signaled a quick refusal. Before long, the stench of urine mixed with the smell of stale sweat made my stomach turn over.

The hours dragged by. Judit and I huddled together, holding hands. I must have dozed off on the hard floor, for a sudden, loud clanging startled me. I looked around and saw that the wide steel gates leading into the warehouse were being pushed open. A dozen figures were silhouetted against the outside brightness. I shaded my eyes to see them.

The sea of prisoners parted in front of a slightly built man with an air of quiet authority. He was dressed in a long, black coat, gray fedora, and hiking boots. He was carrying a brown rucksack in his right hand. It was the man we'd met in Percel Street. Close behind him was a burlier companion, similarly dressed. The second man was carrying a large megaphone under his arm. They were surrounded by eight armed Arrow Cross guards. The group stopped in the middle of the crowd, and the cavernous room grew still.

"I am Raoul Wallenberg from the Swedish embassy," announced the first man through the megaphone. He was speaking in a heavily accented but easily understood Hungarian. "I am here to identify all Swedish citizens. Those of you with a Schutz-Pass in your possession will be released immediately."

I patted my coat pocket. The bulge made by the document was comforting under my fingers, but Judit's sudden intake of breath reminded me that she didn't have any Swedish papers. A desperate murmur broke out in the crowd.

"What about the rest of us?" an old woman cried.

"Please help my child! Please help my baby!" begged a wild-eyed young woman in a tweed coat. She held her baby in Wallenberg's direction.

The noise of the crowd grew louder. I saw an Arrow Cross guard smile and make slicing motions across his throat. Wallenberg waved his hands for quiet. His face was a study in sorrow.

"I am very sorry, but I can't help the rest of you. I have no authority," he said in a quiet voice. "But I do have the authority to acquire the immediate release of all Swedish subjects," he added firmly. "All Swedish citizens, anybody with a Schutz-Pass, please line up along that wall." He pointed to the far end of the room. Only then did I notice that a long wooden table and two chairs had been set up under the grimy windows. Wallenberg and his companion walked over to the table and sat down. The Swede opened up his rucksack and took out a black ledger and a fountain pen.

Those with Schutz-Passes separated from the rest of the crowd and began to form a line.

"You'd better go and line up with them," Judit said, trying to smile through her tears. "Let me give you a hug for good luck!"

Someone behind me jostled me. I lurched forward, stepping on my friend's foot.

"Ouch!"

"Sorry!"

"Not your fault," Judit said. "These slippers aren't good for much." Her toes showed through the ragged material. We looked at each other for a long moment. The lack of good shoes meant frozen toes, and the inability to walk meant almost certain death. If a prisoner could not keep up with the crowd, the Arrow Cross would shoot the poor wretch. I began to cry and Judit knew why.

"Don't worry about me! I'll be fine." She forced a smile and patted my arm. "Maybe I'll be lucky and they won't make us walk very far."

"No chance of that!" We had both heard rumors of the Arrow Cross forcing their Jewish captives to march long distances under gunpoint until they were ready to drop. Only the fittest won the dubious prize of being handed over to the German authorities.

"I wish my shoes would fit you," I exclaimed in frustration.

"Well, they won't. Not these boats," Judit said. "It's my own fault – I should have remembered my shoes. But don't worry! I'll be fine."

Before I could think, I reached into my pocket and took out the billfold that contained my Schutz-Pass. In the chaos surrounding us, nobody was paying attention as I slipped it into Judit's hand.

"Here! The picture on it is so grainy that nobody will be able to tell it isn't of you," I told her. "Everybody says we look alike."

"Marta, I couldn't!" Judit tried to return the billfold.

I pushed her hand away. "You have to. There's no other way. You won't survive a day's march without proper shoes. At least I have shoes I can walk in."

Judit opened and closed her mouth, but no sound came out. We both knew I was right. I gave her a little shove in the direction of the long column of people waiting to see Wallenberg. Judit nodded reluctantly, handed me her own papers, and hugged me tightly before she was swallowed up by the crowd straining to reach the table against the wall.

I made my way back to the corner where we had been sitting and lowered myself onto my haunches. But I felt lonely, so I stood up again and pushed my way through the crowd, desperate to find someone, anyone familiar. I thought I saw Mrs. Lazar across the huge room and tried to make my way toward her. By the time I crossed the sea of humanity, however, she had disappeared and I found myself at the very back of the throng waiting to see Wallenberg. I stayed where I was. The long line moved at a brisk pace, and I moved along with it. The closer and closer I got to the front, to the Swede sitting at the table, the more panicky I became. If I left the line, I would be deported. If I stayed in the line, I would still be deported since I didn't have my pass. It wasn't until the very moment I reached the front of the line that I knew what had to be done. One of the Arrow Cross youths guarding Wallenberg butted me in the back with the barrel of his rifle to make me move closer. I stumbled and had to grip the edge of the table to prevent myself from falling on top of it.

"Put down your rifle," Wallenberg said to the guard in a quiet, authoritative voice. "Put that gun down immediately."

To my surprise, the guard lowered his weapon with a sheepish expression on his face. After giving the guard a long, cold look, Wallenberg turned his attention to me. His face relaxed into a smile. "I believe we've met before," he said politely. "May I see your Schutz-Pass, please?"

I could only gape at him.

"Your Schutz-Pass, please," he repeated patiently.

"I lost my Schutz-Pass on the way here," I managed to croak. "It was in my pocketbook. One of the Arrow Cross took it away from me back at our apartment house when they rounded us up."

"Lying Jew!" cried the soldier standing next to the table. He lifted his rifle into the air, ready to smash it down on my head. I lifted my hands to cover my face and began to pray under my breath. The blow did not fall.

"Stop or I'll report you to your superiors!" thundered Wallenberg. "I demand you put down your gun!"

To my surprise, for the second time, the guard obeyed.

Wallenberg turned back to me. "It's unfortunate you lost your papers, but I'm certain that we have a record of you in my ledger. We keep track of all of our Swedish subjects. What is your name, please?"

I suddenly realized that I couldn't tell him my name. Judit had already used my Schutz-Pass. There was no sign of her, so I was quite certain she had already been released. I tried to think of another name to use, but in my panic I came up blank. There were only two names in the whole, wide world that I could remember – Judit's and mine.

"I am Judit Grof," I whispered.

"Judit Grof . . . Let me see," Wallenberg said. He turned a few pages in his ledger and ran his finger down the page.

I had to remind myself to breathe.

"Judit Grof . . . Yes, here you are. Right between Izsak Funk and Eszter Gross," he said pleasantly. "Please join the others." He pointed to a large group being led toward the open gates by three Arrow Cross guards. Three others were silhouetted in the doorway against the sunny sky.

"Where is this girl's name? Show me her name in your ledger! I don't believe she is in your book! The girl is a liar!" The guard reached for Wallenberg's ledger. The Swede slammed his book shut.

"How dare you question me?" he said coldly. "How dare you! This girl is a Swedish subject. She is no concern of yours! She is one of my Jews. I will report your behavior to your commandant!"

The guard hesitated for an instant before turning his back on us. "To hell with you both!" he muttered. "Who cares about a lying Jew!"

"Hurry up, girl, or your group will be gone," Wallenberg said.

"Thank you! Thank you very much," I mouthed to him.

I ran toward the exit. The armed guards in the doorway stepped aside, and the sunshine blinded me.

· 12 ·

Rose Hill

The uneasy days blended into one another. For the one hour we were allowed out of our houses, we rushed from store to empty store trying to find food, dodging the Arrow Cross at every step. Had we ever had any other life? Only when I flexed my toes and felt the bump made by my grandmother's necklace under my foot could I remember how things used to be – my friends at school, my family at the dinner table, Papa in his office and Mama busy with her charity work, Ervin teasing me until I could have screamed, and Grandmama baking me a special sweet when I visited her.

One cold November morning, we were awakened by thunderous knocking on our apartment door. We hastily pulled robes over our nightclothes.

"What now?" Aunt Miriam asked. Being disturbed and

rounded up by the authorities had become an almost daily occurrence.

"Open the door, Marta," Mama said wearily.

Szasz, the caretaker, was standing in the hallway impatiently tapping his foot. He was accompanied by a young couple in country clothes. They entered our apartment without greeting us. Szasz began to show the young man and his wife around our home.

"As you can see, Mr. Kovacs," he said, "it's a bright and spacious suite. Much too good for these Jews."

The man in the country clothes had the grace to look shame-faced, but his wife held her sharp nose even higher in the air.

"The kitchen is a little small," she said.

"But well furnished," Szasz answered. "Let's look around some more. The stove is in good condition and the icebox is almost new. All the furniture is top quality. I could probably get much higher rent," he added. "Soon they will all be gone."

The woman's brow was furrowed. "What do you think, Tibi?" she asked her husband in a country accent. "Should we take it?"

"Seems fine to me," the man grunted. He avoided looking at me.

The woman turned to Szasz. "We'll rent the suite. When can we move in?"

"This afternoon would be just fine," the super said.

"What about us?" Mama protested. "Where are we supposed to go?"

"This is my home," Aunt Miriam added quietly. "The furniture was given to me by my mother-in-law."

Szasz spat on the kitchen floor. "I want all of you to get out of here immediately," he cried. "And make sure you take none of the furniture with you. Not a single blessed object! Be grateful I didn't report you to the Arrow Cross, thieving Jews!"

I finally found my voice. "But you can't . . ." I wanted to explain that he couldn't evict us without a valid reason, that it was totally unfair.

"Shut up!" Szasz shouted at me. "Shut up! I'll be back with the Arrow Cross if you're not gone."

Once again we bundled up the remnants of our former lives. It took us two hours of trudging to arrive at the white apartment building on Rose Hill, on the Buda side of the Danube. Father had grown up in this cozy apartment. I had wonderful memories of Friday night dinners, with the whole family gathered around a dining-room table groaning with all kinds of delicacies.

"I am certain Ida and Tamas will put us up," my mother said. "Grandmama charged them little rent. I heard them tell her how grateful they were."

"They sound like good people," Aunt Miriam said.

I had met Colonel Nagy and his wife before. I remembered a middle-aged man in an army uniform and his fussily dressed wife taking tea with my grandmother.

Mrs. Nagy answered the door on the first knock. We entered the airy marble foyer.

"Kornelia, Miriam, and young Marta too! How nice!" she said with a strained smile.

Mama explained our situation. "So you see, Ida, we have nowhere else to go. We are desperate. Could we stay with you for a few days until we make other arrangements?"

"Of course you can!" She walked over to the parlor door and opened it wide. "Wait here," she said. "I'll go for Tamas. He's getting a haircut." Without giving us the opportunity to respond or to ask why she didn't just telephone for her husband, she was gone.

As we waited and waited on my grandmother's stiff sofas, my stomach growled. We hadn't eaten all day. I hoped that Mrs. Nagy would share her rations with us when she returned.

"What's taking her so long? I'm famished!" I whined.

"Patience, Marta, patience. Everything takes time. Ida and Tamas will be here soon."

Finally, we heard the key turning in the front door. A burly Arrow Cross officer stood in the doorway. Mrs. Nagy was a few steps behind him. The ferocious expression on her face had turned her into a stranger. I was proud of my mother and my aunt, however; neither of them showed any surprise. Only her quick intake of breath betrayed Aunt Miriam's fear. I realized for the first time that silence could speak.

"So, Ida, you've finally come back – and you brought company too," Mama said sweetly.

Mrs. Nagy's glance was full of contempt. "These are the wretches I told you about," she said. "Get them out of my apartment!"

"You must let us go," Mama said. "We have Swedish protective passports." She took our Schutz-Passes out of her purse and handed them to the Arrow Cross guard. I was grateful I had thought to get mine back from Judit.

He examined our documents intently. "I've heard of these, but I haven't seen one before," he said. "Still, I have my orders from Comrade Szalasi!" He took our passports and tore them into small pieces. We were too shocked even to protest. Mrs. Nagy laughed.

The soldier hustled us outside at gunpoint. We were not allowed to take our belongings. A green police riot vehicle was parked by the front door, and a young policeman was leaning against the truck, smoking a cigarette. When he saw us, he stubbed it out and carefully put the butt into his pocket.

"Take us to the Mirabel," the Arrow Cross said to him.

We climbed into the back of the truck and sat down on one of the wooden benches. The Arrow Cross jumped up after us and sat down on the bench facing us. The vehicle started to move away while Mrs. Nagy watched from the gate. The expression on her face made my blood boil. Just as we were about to turn the corner, I jumped up, leaned out of the truck, and waved my fist at her.

"God will punish you for what you have done!" I cried at the top of my lungs.

The truck turned the corner before I could see her reaction.

In twenty minutes, we arrived at the sleekly modern, gray Mirabel Hotel, which was built into the side of a mountain in Buda. It was now the Hungarian Gestapo headquarters. As we walked into the elegant lobby, I remembered the last time I had visited the hotel. We were celebrating Mama's thirty-fifth birthday with espresso coffee for the adults, cocoa for the children, and sugary cakes for everyone. No cakes would be awaiting us at the end of this journey. The Arrow Cross officer left us, and the armed driver, quiet but not unkind, led us down the steep servants' staircase into the belly of the hotel. We walked through a long, gray maze until the policeman finally stopped in front of a dilapidated brown door, which he opened with an old-fashioned metal key. We found ourselves in a cell-like room with worn carpeting and stained walls. Everything reeked of mildew. Barred windows sat high up on the wall at street level. They were so grimy that hardly any sunlight could penetrate them.

The policeman left the room and we settled on the floor, trying to find some comfort by leaning against the walls.

"Charming place," Mama said.

"Well, at least our problem of finding somewhere to sleep tonight has been solved," said my aunt.

I nestled against Mama, my head resting on her shoulder. Softly, she hummed a lullaby. I must have dozed off, for the opening of the cell door startled me. The young policeman who had driven us to the Mirabel stood in the doorway, towering over us. He held a rifle in one hand and a package wrapped in a newspaper in the other. We shrank against the wall to get as far away from him as possible. The officer leaned his rifle against the wall and quietly closed the door. Although he was a large and heavy man, he crouched down to face us.

I said the first thing that came into my mind: "Did you come to kill us?"

"Don't be daft, girl," said the officer. "I won't hurt you."

He opened the package he was carrying and unwrapped three thick slices of dark bread and three red apples, which he handed to us.

"Quiet, now," he warned us. "I don't know which of my colleagues sympathize with the Arrow Cross."

"What are they planning to do with us?" Mama asked between ravenous munches. "Where are they taking us?"

The policeman hesitated before answering. "I'm not sure," he finally said. "All I know is that every morning, new Jewish prisoners are brought to the hotel. The next morning, they are taken to the trains and then . . ."

His voice trailed off, but he didn't have to continue. All of us knew what the trains meant.

Just then, the door of the cell opened and the Arrow Cross who had arrested us came in with a revolver in his hand. The food in my mouth turned to sawdust and I shoved the remaining bread up my sleeve.

"What are you doing here?" the Arrow Cross asked the policeman.

"I thought I heard some noise coming from this cell, so I came to investigate," the policeman said. "I was wrong. These Jews were sleeping when I got here. What can I do for you, sir?"

The officer dismissed his offer with a wave of his hand. "We need help in the kitchen," he said. "Are you bitches good cooks?"

"Please, sir, my daughter is an excellent cook, much better than either of us," Mama said.

"That's true," Aunt Miriam added. "She is the best."

The officer looked me over. "I don't believe you," he

said. "The girl is way too young and scrawny. Handcuff the other two!" he ordered the policeman.

Within minutes, Mama and Aunt Miriam were being marched out of our cell at gunpoint. Mama's voice rang in my ears as the cell door shut behind them. "Give Marta a chance! Please give her a chance! She is a much better cook than I am."

At dawn, I was loaded into the back of an army truck full of Jewish men and women. We were headed for the trains at the Jozsefvarosi railway station. There was nowhere to sit, but the pressure of the swaying bodies surrounding me kept me upright. The trip took more than an hour because two tires of the truck blew. The young Jewish laborer who was our driver took an unusually long time changing them, despite the Arrow Cross guards' violent threats.

"The boys from the Resistance must have punctured the tires," whispered a woman standing next to me.

"With some luck, we might miss the train," came her companion's heartfelt reply.

We did. The train was pulling out of the station when we arrived. To the accompaniment of our guards' foul curses, our truck turned around and headed back to the Mirabel Hotel.

The next morning, we were less fortunate. Our keepers herded us into a truck at an even earlier hour, and this time the trains were waiting when we got there. The engine was hissing and spewing smoke like a dragon come to life. Hundreds of people with yellow stars were waiting in front of the train. The Arrow Cross handed our group over to armed SS guards who divided us into four groups and lined us up in front of four adjacent boxcars.

"Adolf Eichmann is here," someone said. The news traveled through the crowd as rapidly as a brush fire devours dried grass. All of us had heard of the notorious head of the Gestapo's Jewish office in Hungary. It was well known that Eichmann had made the deportation of the Hungarian Jews his own personal project.

The Arrow Cross guards slid open the steel doors of the cattle cars. As the train whistle blew, the engine belched more smoke and a man at the front of our group was ordered to climb into the boxcar.

"Stop! Halt! Stop! Halt!" The speaker spoke Hungarian with an accent. All of us looked in the direction of the voice. A long, low-slung black car was just pulling into the station behind the train. A man whose features were obscured by a black fedora was hanging out the window. The instant the car stopped, he climbed out, closely followed by a companion. Both of them walked rapidly toward us.

"I am Raoul Wallenberg of the Swedish embassy," he called. "Some of these people are Swedish citizens! You have no authority over them! Release them immediately!"

I could see the indecision come over our guards' faces. "We're just following orders," the leader of the group blustered. "You must speak to Obersturmbannführer Eichmann," he added defensively, pointing in the direction of the only passenger car on the train.

Wallenberg and his companion marched away. For a moment, thin, ordinary, sharp-nosed Adolf Eichmann was visible as he leaned out of his car. Wallenberg climbed into the train and his companion waited on the platform. Everyone – even our guards – waited in suspense. A few minutes later, the Swede reappeared and jumped to the ground. Eichmann was right behind him, once again poking his head out of the train.

"Laß seine Juden gehen! Alle fünfzig!" he thundered crossly in German. A murmur ran through the crowd. Our guards looked stunned.

"What did he say?" I asked a woman standing next to me.

"He said, 'Let his Jews go,'" she translated. "'All fifty of them,'" she added more soberly. At least four hundred Jewish prisoners were waiting on the platform.

Wallenberg strode down the cement path beside the groups of Jewish prisoners. One of the armed SS officers was hot on his heels, counting the number of prisoners being selected by the Swede. Wallenberg pointed to different people as he passed them. "Release him. Release her. Let the child go. I remember issuing her a Schutz-Pass. They're mine! Let them go!" he kept repeating. I noticed that all of the prisoners he chose were either young people or mothers with children.

Finally, Wallenberg stopped in front of our group. When he glanced at me, I saw recognition in his eyes. He pointed his finger at me. "Let her go! She is one of mine. I recognize her face."

"*Fünfzig!* That's fifty prisoners!" said the SS guard. He spoke Hungarian more fluently than the Swede.

Wallenberg nodded his head. His gaze swept over the long column of patiently waiting prisoners who were not chosen. His face was full of sorrow.

The guards grudgingly loaded Wallenberg's "Swedish subjects" back into the army truck that had brought us. As we left the station, the departing train whistle sounded a forlorn farewell.

The Swede's car followed our truck to make sure that we would be let go. We were released when we arrived at the Mirabel. The policeman who had been kind to us was standing guard in front of the hotel.

"Could you please take me to my mother and my aunt? They're working in the kitchen," I asked him.

"They were taken away. I don't know where they are," he said. He looked at me kindly. "You'd better get out of here while you can."

I broke into a run. I had to reach Judit and her mother. I was certain they would put me up. They might even know where I could find Mama and Aunt Miriam.

· 13 ·

Death March

The caretaker was nowhere in sight when I slunk through the iron gates leading to our yellow-star house. I climbed to the third floor and rang Judit's doorbell. There was no answer. I went down the hall to our old apartment and knocked on the door. It felt strange trying to gain admittance to Aunt Miriam's home. No answer there either, so I banged on the door with all my might. It opened suddenly, and the man with the country accent stood in the doorway.

"What do you want?" he asked, keeping his eyes fixed on the floor.

"I'm looking for our friends the Grofs, from down the hall. Would you happen to know where they are?"

"As a matter of fact, I do. A few days after you left, I was returning from the shops when a man came to see them. I overheard their conversation – not that I was snooping," he said defensively.

"Of course not."

"I didn't catch the name of their visitor, but the fellow spoke in Hungarian with a strange accent. He must have been some kind of a foreigner. He was young and slightly built. I heard him tell your friends that he would move them into a house at 2 St. Stephen Park, that they would be safe there."

"Thank you for the information. You've been helpful."

The man's expression softened. "You'd better go before my wife gets back." He blushed deeply. "I'm sorry we took your apartment, but if we hadn't moved in, somebody else would be here instead of us. The sensible thing was to take it, wasn't it?" he asked. When I didn't reply, he closed the door in my face.

It had begun to rain by the time I reached St. Stephen Park. A blue-and-yellow flag fluttered from the roof of an apartment house on the other side of the park. It must be the flag of Sweden, I said to myself. I broke into a quick trot, mindless of the beating, icy rain. I had to circle the park. If I was caught crossing it, I would be deported.

I ran, dodging the ruts and potholes in the bomb-scarred road. Suddenly, I stepped into a large hole, tearing my stocking and scraping my knee. Two more houses to go to safety! I increased my pace. Then, out of nowhere, two Arrow Cross with pointed rifles barred my path. A small black army truck with its motor running held two more Arrow Cross.

"Stop, Jewish filth! Where do you think you're going in such a hurry?" the older of the two men asked.

"I live in that house, sir," I said, pointing to the house with the flag. "I was going home."

"We'll take you to a better place," his comrade said.

The two men looked at each other and burst out laughing. They dragged me into the truck, and the colorful flag quickly became a postage stamp against the glowering sky.

We soon arrived at the racetrack. When Ervin and I once came here with Papa, there had been splendid silks and prancing horses and glamorous spectators. Now there were hundreds of young women and girls with six-pointed stars on their clothing. They were milling about on the gigantic field, with guards in Arrow Cross uniforms and SS soldiers with drawn rifles surrounding them. I looked around to see if there was anyone I knew.

"Marta! Marta! Is it you?" A familiar voice. Judit flung her arms around my neck.

"Why are we here? I was told you had moved to St. Stephen Park. To a safe house. I was trying to get to your place when I was arrested."

"I *was* in St. Stephen Park," Judit replied. "And thank God, as far as I know, Mother is still there. Mr. Wallenberg came to our old block right after you were forced to leave. He issued us Schutz-Passes and then he moved us to a Swedish house in St. Stephen Park. He told us there are other Swedish houses in the Jewish district, and Swiss houses too. Both the Swedish and the Swiss embassies have secretly bought up a lot of buildings and declared them to be a part of Sweden or Switzerland. Jewish people in these houses are under their protection. Neither the Hungarians nor the Germans can touch them."

"Then how come you're here?"

"Because I'm stupid, that's why."

"Seriously. What happened?"

"I'm ashamed to tell you. You won't believe it, it's so foolish."

"Tell me."

She sighed. "You must have noticed that the road in St. Stephen Park is full of potholes."

I pointed to my torn stocking. "I noticed too late and now my leg aches."

"Yesterday morning, the horse of an Arrow Cross officer stepped into a deep hole in the road and broke his leg, right in front of our house," Judit said. "I saw it happen through my window. The poor horse was neighing and whining. It was in a lot of pain. When the Arrow Cross rider saw how his horse was suffering, he shot it in the head. As soon as the shot rang out, people rushed to carve some meat off the horse. There was such a crowd that I decided not to waste any time by getting my Schutz-Pass. I was afraid the horse would get stripped of all of its meat before I got to it. I grabbed a bowl and a large knife in the kitchen and ran out to the street," she explained. "Before I could even get close to the horse, however, its owner demanded to see my papers. He refused to listen to my explanations and flagged down a German truck. The Nazis brought me here."

"Have you heard why we are here?"

"The rumor is that the Germans are collecting younger Jewish women to dig ditches. The ditches are supposed to stop the Soviet tanks from reaching Budapest."

"Not if they count on us to dig them. Look at us!"

Judit began to laugh. Both of us were as thin as scarecrows.

"Oh, I hope the Soviets will get here soon!" she said fervently.

"They've got to!" I replied.

The gray autumn rain fell as we trudged along the old Danube road leading to Vienna. We were two waves in a sea of Jewish women belonging to the sisterhood of the yellow star. Although a curtain of rain dulled the beauty of the angry river snaking alongside the road, it could not blunt my fear. I was soaked through to the skin but barely felt it. All I could think about were my mother and my aunt. Where were they? What was happening to them? I knew that Judit's anxiety must have matched mine because she kept casting frantic glances in my direction. We were completely silent, afraid even to whisper to each other. Numbed, we trudged along. Stopping for even a moment to catch our breath would have meant permanent rest among the dead at the side of the road.

I lost track of time. Only a few weeks had passed since Judit and I met at the racetrack, but it seemed as if we had been digging ditches forever, first on the outskirts of Budapest, now on the road leading to the town of Hegyeshalom, on the Austrian border. It was back-breaking work. Our clothing was in tatters and our skin had become gray from ingrained dirt. Every day we worked in the trenches for ten hours before being herded into a large column to march, exhausted, for six more long hours toward the border, where the German authorities were waiting for us. Our ultimate destination was a work camp in Germany.

We were dirty, tired, and rarely looked up, for we were focused on the groaning of our bellies and the sheer physical effort needed to keep moving. At night we stopped in outdoor arenas or in schoolyards, where we slept like animals on wet straw strewn on the ground. Sometimes there wasn't even any straw, and we would lie on damp earth or cold stone.

The days and nights had become formless. By the time we saw the church spires of Komarom outlined in the distance, we were so exhausted that we didn't even have the strength to offer words of consolation to each other. All I longed for was a pile of hay where I could rest my head and our daily serving of watery soup to calm my belly. All my fight was gone. I was ready to give up, whatever the consequences, when suddenly, miraculously, the movie of my imagination switched on. I was transported back to my old home, to my familiar room with its lacy curtains catching the moonbeams. I was still a little girl with my hair in plaits, lying in my bed, waiting for Mama and Papa to come into my room to bless me as they did every Shabbos eve.

Then came the nightmare. I remembered Mama being taken away, Ervin and Gabor being marched out of our building's courtyard at gunpoint, Grandmama lying on the floor with the trickle of blood running down the side of her face. And Papa, so far away, building roads somewhere in Yugoslavia. I thought of Papa and the way he used to be before the war – so good, so clever, so kind. He was always so gentle with me, so careful even when he was removing a sliver from my finger.

"My darling Papa," I called into the beating, icy rain.

A sudden noise caused me to turn. I was just in time to see the woman who had been walking behind me throw herself into the deep ditch running along the roadside. She was swallowed up by the scrubby vegetation. The guards did not notice.

"I'm going to jump into the ditch! Come with me!" I whispered to Judit.

She shook her head vehemently. "No, don't be crazy! It's too risky. They'll kill you!"

"It's our only chance!"

"You're making a terrible mistake," Judit said.

With a last glance in her direction, I gathered up my remaining strength and threw myself into the ditch. As I rolled down the steep bank, a thorny branch scraped my face. I pushed it back, careful not to disturb the protective canopy of bushes. Then I lay motionless in the ditch for what seemed an eternity. At first, I heard the heavy thumping of the feet of the passing prisoners on the road above me. Then came a silence that was broken only by the whistling of the wind.

I had no idea how much time had passed when a loud rustling noise to my left caused my heart to race. Could the sounds have come from a wolf roaming the countryside? I sat up. A sheepdog was staring right at me. He was so close that I could see the doleful expression in his eyes even in the dusk. When I stretched out a cautious hand to scratch him behind a floppy ear, he gave me a soggy lick on my nose. Suddenly, the world seemed a less harsh place.

"Oh, you beauty! Did you come to keep me company?"

I was answered with an energetic wagging of his tail.

When I stood up, it took several moments for the pins and needles in my hands and feet to disappear. I climbed the banks of the ditch to the narrow road stretching beside it. The countryside was eerily empty, except for a large crow hopping about in the dirt a few feet away. There was no sign of the woman who had thrown herself into the ditch before me.

I began to breathe a little easier. What to do next? Which way should I go? The decision was taken out of my hands when an army truck appeared around a bend in the road. The mournful tones of the German song "Lili Marlene" wafted out into the chilly autumn air. The sheep-dog gave a frightened yelp and scurried away. The truck was coming closer. It was too late for me to dive back into the ditch. I had to get rid of the yellow star on my jacket. There was no time to tear it off as I had done before, however, so I ripped off my coat instead and threw it into the ditch. I was grateful for the dusk and quite certain that neither the driver nor his passengers had been able to see what I was doing. I brushed off the twigs still clinging to my skirt, smoothed down my hair as best I could, then stood hugging myself to ward off the chilly air, waiting for the truck to reach me. When it was only a few feet away, I started waving my arms and jumping up and down. The truck came to a screeching halt. There was a large swastika decorating the wagon's tarpaulin. A uniformed German soldier was at the wheel.

I forced a smile to my face. "Heil Hitler! Long live Szalasi!" I babbled over my outstretched arm. "Thank God you're here!"

The driver's arm shot out in response. "Heil Hitler!" he barked, then began shouting at me in German.

"No *Deutsch*! I don't speak German."

I must have been more convincing than I realized, for the soldier merely gave an irritated shrug and repeated, in halting Hungarian: "Who are you, girl? Where are you going?"

"My name is Anna Nagy. I am from Komarom." It wasn't hard to force myself to cry. "I was bombed out of my house. It burned to the ground. My whole family was killed." I forced a louder sob. "I was almost killed by a falling beam myself. I was hoping to hitch a ride to Budapest, where my auntie lives. Please help me!"

The driver seemed satisfied by my torn clothing, dirty face, disheveled hair. A second soldier, who couldn't have been more than two or three years older than I was, was leaning out of the back of the truck, listening to what we were saying.

"Show me your papers, girl," the driver growled.

I began to cry even harder. "My papers were burned with everything else. I don't even have a coat." I wiped away my tears with knuckles that were gray from digging ditches.

The driver scratched his head.

"Oh, come on, Hans," said the second soldier to the driver in a good-natured voice. "The poor girl has gone through enough already. She can get her documents replaced in Budapest." He spoke Hungarian more fluently than the driver.

I held my breath. Finally, the driver nodded.

"Hop in, Anna," the second soldier said. He held out his hand and hoisted me into the back of the truck. I knocked against him as the driver revved up the motor and continued on his route.

As my eyes became accustomed to the darkness, I looked around the interior. I could just make out the outline of a bulky figure huddled in the corner of the truck, using a knapsack for a seat. The person's features were obscured.

"Anna, let me introduce you to my comrade," the soldier said jauntily.

The figure edged closer until I found myself looking into the dead eyes of the SS guard who had made sure that Wallenberg took no more than fifty prisoners off the train at the Jozsefvarosi railway station. I screwed my eyes shut and shook my head. I told myself that such coincidences did not happen, that all of this had to be a nightmare. When I opened my eyes again, the SS man from the transport was still beside me. I prayed he wouldn't recognize me.

"I know I've seen you before, but where?" he muttered in a puzzled manner. Finally, his face contorted into a foxy grin. "I remember where I've seen you, Jewish slut. No

Jew-loving Swede will save your skin this time!" Then he spat right in my face.

"What's the matter with you, Hermann?" the young German soldier asked. "Have you gone crazy?"

"Do you know who this is?" The SS soldier interrupted him. "She isn't anybody called Anna. She isn't from Komarom. She is a cursed Jew! A couple of weeks ago, she was taken off my transport by that Jew-loving Wallenberg."

By now, the first soldier's revolver was pointed at my head, although I thought I could detect a glimmer of pity in his eyes. I gathered together the remnants of my courage.

"Please, please don't betray me!" I begged. "Please help me! I'll make it worth your while."

A cunning expression came over the SS guard's cruel face. "What will you give us if we let you go?" he asked. "All of you Jews are filthy rich."

"Something you can sell. Something that's worth several months' salary."

"Stop lying, bitch!" he snarled. "It won't help you."

The younger soldier also seemed unconvinced, but he lowered his gun nevertheless. "What have you got, girl?" he asked.

I crouched down, pulled off my left shoe, took out the insole, and pulled out Grandmama's necklace. The gold star glimmered in the semi-darkness. "A necklace. It's real gold. It'll fetch a lot of money if you sell it." I held it out. He grabbed it out of my hand and greedily examined it.

"Look at that! She was telling the truth," the younger soldier said.

"It's Jew garbage!"

"Don't be stupid, Hermann. It's gold. It must be valuable," said his comrade.

"I assure you it is. Now it's yours. Please let me go!"

"Are you crazy?" the SS guard snapped. "Why, we wouldn't let you go even if –"

"Hermann, you're wrong!" the young soldier said. "We can't shoot her. Hans would want to know why, and we don't want anyone to know we took her gold. She can't be trusted to keep quiet, so we have to let her go. Let me see her necklace."

The SS guard gave it to him reluctantly. The soldier tore off the Star of David pendant and put the gold chain into his pocket. Then he leaned out of the back of the truck and threw the medallion into the darkening fields on the side of the road.

"Nobody will find that Jew star out there," he said before knocking on the small window in the partition that separated the driver from us.

The driver looked back and the soldier motioned to him to pull up at the side of the road. After he had stopped, the driver slid aside the pane of glass.

"What's wrong?" he asked.

"The girl is getting carsick. She wants to walk," the soldier said.

I felt a deep sense of satisfaction when I saw the SS guard's fuming face as I jumped out of the truck.

I traveled only at night, without a coat, in the freezing autumn weather. In the daytime, I hid in haystacks or ditches. On the fourth day of my journey, an occasional snowflake whitened my hair, and I realized that December was around the corner. Twice I was lucky enough to come across some wild berries still growing on a few bushes so late in the season. The rest of the time I went hungry. It took me five days to reach the outskirts of Budapest. I decided to return to 2 St. Stephen Park. Perhaps Mrs. Grof would have news of Mama and Aunt Miriam.

· 14 ·

Reunion

I was so filthy and wretched that I was barely recogniz-able by the time I arrived at the wrought-iron gates of 2 St. Stephen Park. My hair was a matted bush covering my face. My skirt was in tatters and my gray stockings were filthy and bloody from the scratches on my legs. Fortu-nately, the lowering clouds not only obscured the moon, but also hid me from hostile eyes. Through the darkness I could still see the outline of the Swedish flag on the roof.

I rang the doorbell. Its piercing tone cut the blackness and I was sure I had woken up all the inhabitants of the building. I cowered against the rough stucco wall, expect-ing the barrel of a gun in the small of my back. Instead, the gates creaked open and two young men stepped out. I could see the outlines of the revolvers they held in their hands.

"Halt! Who is there?" the first man asked.

"Where do you think you're going?" the second said.

My heart almost stopped from joy. Was I hallucinating? No! I knew what I had just heard.

"Who is there?" the first man repeated.

"Ervin! Gabor! Thank God it's you! It's me, Marta! Don't you recognize me?"

A quick intake of breath. "Shh, be quiet! The darkness has ears!" Ervin whispered.

Gabor grasped my arm and pushed me through the gates, clicking the doors closed behind us. Ervin pulled me close for a quick embrace. His cheek felt moist against my face.

"Follow us!" he whispered.

We climbed four flights of slippery steps, then turned into a narrow hallway where we picked our way around dozens of people lying on the floor. Some had blankets, but most were unprotected against the cold cement.

"Careful, don't step on anyone," Gabor whispered.

We came to the last door at the end of the hall, stepped over a sleeping child blocking the doorway, and went in.

"What are you —"

"Shh! You'll wake everybody! There will be time to explain everything later." Ervin shone his flashlight on the parquet floor. Every inch of space was covered by sleeping bodies. A baby began to stir and moan as the light touched his face. Ervin quickly turned off his flashlight and pulled me after him. Gabor was so close behind that I could feel his breath fanning my neck. Finally, we went into another room.

As soon as the door clicked closed behind us, Ervin turned on the lights. It was so good to see his face again. When I looked around, I saw we were in the bathroom of the apartment. Ervin engulfed me in a bear hug so tight that I could hardly breathe. I wanted him never to let me go, and I hugged back as hard as I could. Both of us were laughing and crying at the same time. When we finally came up for air, it was my cousin's turn to embrace me. I was surprised by how tall both boys had become since I last saw them. Ervin even sported the beginnings of a wispy mustache.

"What are you doing here? Have you heard from Mama and Aunt Miriam? Where are they? Are they all right? What happened to you?" The words tumbled out of my mouth.

"What about you? Why are you so thin and pale?" Ervin asked with a worried frown.

"Whoa! Stop it!" Gabor interjected. "One person at a time. First, let me get you some food, Marta. You look like you could use it."

"I *am* famished."

Gabor slipped out of the room and brought back a slice of dark bread and a boiled potato. I sat down on the toilet lid and the boys perched on the edge of the tub. The food tasted better in my mouth than anything I had eaten before.

"There is so much to talk about," I told them. "But first of all, I want to know if you've heard from Mama and Aunt Miriam. We were taken to Gestapo headquarters at the Mirabel. The Arrow Cross separated us. They took them to work in the kitchen. Do you know if they're still there?"

A worried look passed between the boys.

"What's wrong?"

"Mama and Aunt Miriam were taken to the Ghetto," Ervin said.

"The Ghetto? What do you mean?"

"A couple of weeks ago, all Jews were ordered to move into a walled-in ghetto behind the synagogue on Dohany Street," Gabor explained. "Only those of us who live in Swedish or Swiss safe houses are left outside."

"The Ghetto is a terrible place, Marta," Ervin said. "If you saw it for yourself, you wouldn't believe it. It's incredibly overcrowded and dirty, with dead bodies piled up everywhere like firewood. There is no food, no running water, no electricity. People are starving to death."

"How can Mama and Aunt Miriam survive?"

Ervin held my hand tightly while dry sobs shook my body. When I grew calmer, he added, "Peter is with the Resistance. He told us that Resistance fighters are smuggling in a little bit of food and water in Red Cross trucks, but it's not nearly enough."

"Peter! Where is he?"

"He'll be here tomorrow morning," Ervin said.

"Is he all right? What has happened to him?"

"Peter is fine," Ervin said. "It's safer for you not to know everything."

"Please!"

Ervin cracked his knuckles and wouldn't answer.

"Come on," Gabor said. "She's entitled to know." He turned to me. "After he came back from Pecs, Peter received his conscription notice. His parents threw him out of the house when he told them he wouldn't fight for Hungary. His mother didn't speak up for him, not even when his father called him a traitor and told him he never wanted to see him again."

"That hurt Peter the most," Ervin said.

"Poor Peter! He must have been devastated!"

"He hasn't seen them since," Gabor said. "He knew of Sam Stein's involvement with the Resistance. Sam hooked him up with them, and he's been with them ever since."

"Your Peter is a brave person," Ervin said. "He saved our lives. He helped us escape from the Arrow Cross."

"Tell me everything."

"So much has happened that I don't even know where to begin," Ervin said.

"The beginning."

"After we were caught, Gabor and I were sent to dig ditches in Yugoslavia. Adam was separated from us. We don't know what happened to him."

"Oh God, poor Mrs. Grof!"

"She doesn't know about Adam," Gabor said. "She seems to have disappeared. We've been asking, but nobody knows where she is." He stood up and rubbed his back. "This seat is too hard." He sat down cross-legged on the tile floor. Ervin sat down beside him before he picked up the thread of Gabor's story.

"In the middle of October, the Arrow Cross brought us back to Budapest. They took us to the synagogue in Dohany Street. It was a madhouse. There were at least a thousand of us crowded together. Arrow Cross soldiers with guns were everywhere, blocking all the exits. They even stood on the staircases leading to the rabbi's pulpit. I was certain that one of the bastards had his gun pointed straight at my head," Ervin said ruefully.

"Ervin and I realized very quickly that we had to get out of there," Gabor said, jumping in. "Just when we thought there was no possible escape, we noticed a tall boy in a Levente uniform. He had a rifle in his hands and a knapsack over his shoulder. He seemed to be explaining something to the Arrow Cross guard and then he waded into the crowd. He pushed his way right to us. We finally got a good look at his face in the dim light. It was Peter! 'Don't say a word!' he whispered in my ear."

"By then, we had caught on," Ervin said. "He started screaming at us at the top of his voice. 'Jewish garbage! You thought you could cheat me? You thought you could get away from me, didn't you? Well, you were wrong! You won't escape me again!' Then he marched us out of the synagogue at gunpoint, pushing and shoving us the whole time. The prisoners parted in front of us much as the Red Sea must have parted in front of Moses. Nobody questioned us, nobody stopped us. It was so easy."

He shifted on the floor and continued speaking. "Once we were outside, we stopped behind a large tree in the yard. Peter took two Levente uniforms from his knapsack. He had everything from boots to caps to revolvers. We pulled the uniforms over our clothes."

"Well, you finally got to wear a Levente uniform," I said sarcastically.

Ervin ignored me. "Nobody noticed what we were doing. When we left, the armed sentry at the gates even waved goodbye."

"What did you do next?"

"There isn't much more to tell," Gabor said. "We found out that most of the Jewish tenants from our old block had been brought here by Mr. Wallenberg, so we moved here too."

"Nowhere is safe any more," Ervin said. "We heard that the Arrow Cross broke into a Swiss house where the Krausz family was staying and shot everybody. It's not even advisable to keep our Schutz-Passes with us all the time. We're saving them for a real emergency, when there is no other way out. I'll show you where we've hidden them."

He crouched down on the floor and reached around the side of the tub. Carefully, he pulled out a small canvas-covered package that was lodged between the tub and the wall. He unwrapped it to reveal the familiar protective passports. "We were told again to send for Mr. Wallenberg if the Arrow Cross soldiers refuse to recognize our Schutz-Passes. Wallenberg takes on the Nazis, and he never loses." Ervin's voice was full of admiration. He slipped the protective passports back into their hiding place.

I told them how our Schutz-Passes had been taken away. "What will happen to me if we need to use our passports?" To my shame, my voice shook.

"Don't worry, Marta. You'll be fine," Gabor said. "God will protect you, and my mother and Aunt Nelly too." His face brightened. "This will be one of the first places they'll look for us when the war is over."

"If they live that long," Ervin said. "Oh, Gabor, when will you open your eyes? How I envy your blindness!"

Gabor did not reply.

It was past midnight when we stopped talking. Ervin and Gabor insisted that I occupy the bathtub while they stretched out on the hard tile floor. I was so exhausted that I fell asleep immediately. At dawn, gunfire woke me.

· 15 ·

The Ghetto

It took us more than an hour to arrive at the Ghetto. The Arrow Cross soldiers who had invaded our hiding place marched us at gunpoint through the December snow. They gave us no time to put on our shoes or coats. We trudged through the cold streets barefoot and freezing. Ahead of me, a gray-haired woman slowed down, unable to keep up with the punishing pace they had set for us. She dropped to the icy road, exhausted. I had barely passed her when the explosion of gunfire behind me spoke of her fate.

I marched beside Ervin and Gabor. My whole being was concentrated on completing the next frozen step and the next after that. Finally, Gabor broke the silence.

"I thought we'd be safe longer," he said.

I hunched my shoulders in a futile attempt to ward off the cold. All I could do was listen to the boys speak.

"I was so wrong," Ervin said. "When we heard what happened to the Krauszes, we should have moved right away."

"Where could we have gone?" Gabor asked. "We had nowhere else to go."

"I should have fetched our Schutz-Passes," Ervin muttered.

"And got shot in the process? They were too quick, and they had too many guns." Gabor turned to me. "How are you holding up, Marta?"

I was too frozen to reply. My steps faltered.

"Let me help you," Ervin said.

The boys linked their arms through mine and dragged me along. When I thought I couldn't take another step, whatever the consequences, we came to a guard's hut in front of the tall wooden fence that surrounded the Ghetto. We were ordered to stop. We sunk to the ground, and Ervin and Gabor warmed my feet with their frozen hands. Life flooded back into my limbs and I slowly became aware of my surroundings. Dozens of Arrow Cross guards with drawn guns patrolled the perimeter of the Ghetto. Three trucks blocked the entrance. A large red cross, the insignia of the International Red Cross, was painted on the side of each of the trucks. Two Arrow Cross in front of the guard hut were arguing with the drivers, telling them to move their trucks.

"Get up, vermin! Get up!" shouted our captors. With the Red Cross now out of the way, they opened the large wooden gates. They herded us into the Ghetto much as a shepherd would drive his recalcitrant sheep in the direction he wanted them to go. But there was a great difference with these shepherds of people: our guards had drawn guns instead of shepherds' crooks.

As I was about to pass through the gates, the red hair of one of the truck drivers caught my eye. There was something familiar about him. He turned his head just as I walked by. It was Sam Stein! I stopped in my tracks so suddenly that a woman behind me bumped into me full force. The flow of the crowd dragged Ervin and Gabor away from me. Sam rolled down the truck's window.

"Tell Peter!" I cried before the swell of people surrounding me swept me into the Ghetto.

I saw Ervin turn and wave his arm in the air. I waved back. The boys pushed their way through the crowd, back to my side. We clung to each other, determined not to be separated again. As soon as I looked around, I realized that we had come into a strange and different place. It was a world teeming with cadaverous, shadowy figures decorated with yellow stars; a world of mountainous piles of garbage spewing an overwhelming stench into the air; a world of corpses piled up like logs in what was once the courtyard of the synagogue on Dohany Street, in Klauzal Square.

At Klauzal Square, we waited to cross the street while

a large group of prisoners who had arrived before us flooded forward. Gone were the swings of my childhood and the wide-open grassy space that was so perfect for flying our kites. Gone were the groups of old men playing chess and the nursemaids running after their mischievous charges. Instead, there were armed SS and Arrow Cross guards everywhere.

The other prisoners were so close to us that we could see and hear the armed guards shoving and kicking and yelling at their victims. I saw a dignified middle-aged woman handing a guard her glistening wedding ring while tears rolled down her cheeks. A well-dressed older man humbly held out his homburg hat. A squealing infant clung to his mother's neck while a brutish guard ripped the diaper off his tender little bottom in search of hidden jewels.

We were lined up in a long column to await our turn to be interviewed by the Arrow Cross.

"What are you hiding, girl?" asked the officer in charge, turning to me.

"Nothing, sir. We weren't allowed to bring any of our belongings with us."

"Idiots," the Arrow Cross murmured under his breath. "Go there." He pointed to a longer queue. I waited and waited until it was my turn to be searched by another guard. I tried to will away his intrusive hands, to blot them out by thinking of Mama and Papa and our family when all of us were together. Eventually, he ordered me to go to building 5, across from Klauzal Square. I walked away slowly, praying for Ervin and Gabor to rejoin me.

"Marta, wait up!" Ervin's voice. Tears of relief ran down my face when I heard that they too had been assigned to building 5.

Building 5 was a tall house with peeling yellow paint. At one time it must have been home to three families, one on each floor. Now it teemed with frightened people.

We picked our way up the stairs to the second floor.

"There is no space to sit," Ervin said.

"The crowd seems to be a little thinner at the far end of the room," Gabor pointed out.

We waded into the bedraggled crowd. No one even spoke when we accidentally disturbed their emaciated bodies with our feet. A tug at my sleeve. I looked down at a ragged, bearded creature sitting on the floor. I had never seen him before.

"Marta Weisz, don't you recognize me?"

His voice was familiar.

"It's me. Sam Lazar."

I crouched down for a better look. The skeletal man bore little resemblance to the jolly Mr. Lazar I remembered.

"Have you seen your mother?" he asked.

"Mama? What do you mean? Where is she?"

He pointed to the ceiling. "She's on the fourth floor."

I hugged him and we made our way to the staircase.

My mother and I saw each other at the same instant. She and my aunt were huddled with another woman in a corner of the grimy hallway. They looked so gray, so worn, so old that my heart wept. Mama struggled to her feet and stumbled toward us, her arms outstretched. We hugged and hugged. I wanted it to last forever. Aunt Miriam was grinning from ear to ear.

"Have you heard any news of my Judit and my Adam?" A timid voice interrupted us. Mama's companion turned her head away from the shadows. It was Mrs. Grof.

"Rachel was the first person we saw when we were brought here," Mama said. "She was picked up by the Arrow Cross while she lined up for food."

"Why aren't Judit and Adam with you?" she asked.

We told her everything we knew. After a long moment, she smiled.

"My Judit and Adam are all right," she said. "I can feel it in my bones. They'll come home when the war is over, you'll see. I can hardly wait to see them!"

None of us answered her.

The three women shifted closer together to make room for us beside them on the floor. There we stayed day after day, without a morsel of food or a drop of water. The days melted into nights, until we lost count. The world around us whirled in a gray haze. Then suddenly, there was Peter. Peter in his Levente uniform. Peter holding a canteen of water to our lips. Peter giving us thick slices of black bread. We fell on the food like ravenous animals.

"Slowly, slowly," he warned. "Eat slowly or you'll be sick."

"What are you doing here?" Ervin asked after the food had revived us.

Peter motioned in the direction of the family sitting closest to our group on the stone floor. They were straining to hear what we were saying. We moved to the head of the stairs, where we couldn't be overheard.

"How did you get in here?" Gabor asked.

Peter laughed. "Getting in is no problem. Getting out – now that's more difficult. I told them at the gate that I had to come into the Ghetto to find the Jews who had cheated me. Exactly the same thing I told the Arrow Cross at the synagogue on Dohany Street. It worked both times." He looked at his watch. "Good. Right at this moment, the guard is changing at the front gate."

Ervin cracked his knuckles. "So?"

"So we'll walk out of the Ghetto together," Peter said. "When Stein told me you were taken into the Ghetto, I went to St. Stephen Park to get your Schutz-Passes. It's a good thing you showed me where you had hidden them, Ervin. I'd already heard that you had been brought here with your sister, Mrs. Weisz," he said to Mama.

"Our Schutz-Passes were torn up by the Arrow Cross," Mama said.

Peter's smile widened. "I have some extras, thanks to Stein and his friends."

He gave me the Schutz-Pass of a girl called Leah Klein. The grainy photograph in the protective passport was so faded that nobody could tell it wasn't me. Mama became Mrs. Ida Klein and Aunt Miriam was Mrs. Eva Singer. There was no Schutz-Pass for Judit's mother.

"Say goodbye to Mrs. Grof," Peter said to Mama and Aunt Miriam. "I didn't know she was with you, so I didn't bring her any documents. I'll come back for her another time."

"Rachel has to come with us," Aunt Miriam protested.

"We can't leave her here. You might not be able to come back," Mama said, sounding every bit as determined as my aunt. "If Rachel doesn't come with us, I cannot leave either."

Mrs. Grof was silent, her hands clenched so tightly in her lap that the tips of her fingers had turned white.

"There is no time for this. We're taking too long," Peter warned. Then he sighed. "Fine! You win! Mrs. Grof can come with us. If anyone asks, I'll say I forgot her papers." He looked at the rest of us questioningly. We nodded our agreement.

We made our way to the front gates of the Ghetto. I was breathing so rapidly that I could hear my blood pounding in my ears. The Arrow Cross guards stationed there stopped us.

"Where are you taking these Jews?" the younger of the two guards asked.

"I was ordered by my platoon leader to escort them out of the Ghetto. They're Swedish citizens," Peter said casually. He handed our Schutz-Passes to the guards. "Here are their documents, comrade."

"What does your platoon leader want with them?" the older Arrow Cross soldier asked.

"I have no idea," Peter said. "I just follow orders."

The second Arrow Cross began to examine our Schutz-Passes. Aunt Miriam moaned quietly, but Mama hushed her. The guard's eyes traveled over us. His face was full of contempt. "What do you think we should do, Fritzi?" he asked his partner. "Should we let them go?"

The first Arrow Cross shrugged his shoulders. "Why not, Jancsi? Who gives a damn about these Jews? The fewer of them there are, the better I like it."

We were already a few feet away from them when the older guard called out, "Halt! You showed us five sets of papers, but there are six Jews with you."

Before Peter could answer, Aunt Miriam suddenly broke away and ran toward the guards.

"Leave us alone! What do you want with us?" she cried.

Peter bolted after her to stop her. Ervin had one arm clasped around Gabor's waist to keep him from running after them as well. His other hand was over Gabor's mouth to stifle his screams. Shots rang out. Aunt Miriam was on the ground, Peter's body draped over hers. They were both dead. I realized with a shock that the keening sounds I was hearing came from my own throat.

Dead! My Peter, dead. It couldn't be. The hand grasping my arm was my mother's, not Peter's. The tears intermingling with mine were my mother's, not Peter's. The sobs I was hearing were coming from my mother's throat, not Peter's. And my aunt – so charming and gay, so kind, so full of life – dead! The thought was inconceivable.

I could hear Ervin screaming at the guards. "What's the matter with you? Are you crazy? We're Swedish citizens. You killed these people for no reason at all. You killed them because your comrade forgot to bring one of our Schutz-Passes. I will get Mr. Wallenberg immediately. He will report you to your superiors."

The younger guard became frightened. "It wasn't our fault. What were we to think?"

"Get out of here!" the older guard cried. "All of you!"

The gates closed behind us.

"Where should we go now?" I asked. It did not seem to matter.

"Back to St. Stephen Park, I suppose," said Ervin.

"But it isn't safe any more."

"The Arrow Cross has already been through it. Besides, what choice is there?" Ervin took Mama's hand and led our forlorn group away from the Ghetto.

When we got back to the safe house, we comforted each other as best as we could, but without much success. Gabor covered his head with a yarmulke. Then, with tears running down his cheeks, he began to pray: "Hear, O Israel, the Lord is our God, the Lord is One."

After Gabor finished reciting the ancient words, Mama put her arm around his shoulders and drew him close to her.

"I had to say the *Shema* for her," he said, sobbing. "There was no time back there for her to say it herself."

The Soviets were advancing, we'd heard, and the war would soon be over. Too late, too late. Peter is forever gone. Aunt Miriam, dead. I'll never see them again, I thought to myself.

·16·

Liberation

The shelves of the grocery stores were completely bare, but Mama had got hold of a sack of dried beans on the black market and she made watery soup out of it. All of us had become skeletal. Ervin and Gabor had to punch new holes into their belts to keep their pants from falling down. The black skirt I had once been so proud of hung loose on me. I had become accustomed to the constant gnawing hunger pains in the pit of my stomach.

We had moved into the kitchen of the apartment at 2 St. Stephen Park. The bathroom had become too small a living space since Mama and Mrs. Grof had joined us. I walked over to the window above the kitchen sink and looked outside. Nobody would have guessed that Christmas was around the corner. The few dour individuals who had ventured outdoors were lean and shabby. They scurried about with frightened expressions on their faces. No laughter, no joy lightened the twilight.

On Christmas Eve, a symphony of drums pounded in the sky. The Soviets had begun a heavy, continuous bombing of Budapest. We were freezing. All heat and electricity had been cut off, and we had no wood for our stoves: we had already chopped up all of the furniture. We had no water. In the entire building only one toilet, down in the basement, was working. If any of us needed to use it, we had to climb down four sets of steep stairs and endure a long queue as we awaited our turn.

The next morning, Christmas Day, we were gathered around the gas stove in the kitchen. We had made a small fire in the tray below the gas rings, and the warmth of the flame felt wonderful over my outstretched fingers. Ervin and I were sitting so close to each other that I could see each individual freckle on his nose. I could also see the small brother I used to play with in the outlines of this gangly stranger. My brother's obnoxious younger self reappeared when I dropped my head nostalgically on his shoulder. He drew away from me.

"Ugh! Your hair reeks!" he cried.

"Thanks a lot. Yours doesn't smell so good either. What am I supposed to do? In case you haven't noticed, we don't have water." I was desperate to wash my hair, but drinking water was our priority.

Mama looked troubled. "We're becoming uncivilized,

like beasts in the jungle. We must get cleaned up somehow. What can we do?"

Gabor had the answer: he organized us into a snow brigade. He put his jacket over his tattered clothing and went into the icy street to fill a pail with snow. He then carried the pail up the front steps, where he passed it to Ervin. Ervin carried the snow up the staircase to the second floor, where he gave it to me. I carried it up to the third floor, where I handed it over to Mama, who took it up to the fourth floor and gave it to Mrs. Grof. Mrs. Grof melted the snow over the mini bonfire below the gas rings and poured the resulting water into the bathtub. We had arranged to use the tub with the married couple who had replaced us in the bathroom. We repeated this process over and over again until the tub was full. We were too weak to carry more than one pail at a time, so filling up the tub took a long time.

"We have enough water for only one bath," Mama said. "We'll have to draw lots to decide the order we'll get to bathe. It's the only fair way."

We put five folded pieces of paper, each marked with a number between one and five, into a hat and drew lots.

"I'm first," Ervin crowed.

"I'm second," Mama said, unsuccessfully trying to hide her pleasure. Before the war, she used to spend hours in her scented bath.

Gabor didn't look too happy about coming third, while Mrs. Grof wore a positively thunderous expression about being fourth. What should I have said, coming last? It was the luck of the draw. There was nothing I could do about it, so I kept quiet.

"Everybody must take a very quick bath, then the water won't cool down too much by the time Rachel and Marta get their turn," Mama said.

My mother was wrong. Gray, cold water awaited me an hour later. I stood there, naked, shivering, staring at the water for a long moment before stepping into the tub. It was so cold it made me shudder, and I had to close my eyes to shut out the sight of the scum floating on top. After a while, however, I began to enjoy myself. We had no soap, but the water felt cool and refreshing against my skin. I was just rinsing my hair when the first shot came whistling through the door, just missing my head. It was followed in the blink of an eye by a second missile that came even closer. A crater appeared in the wall to my left. There was heavy pounding on the door.

"Let me in! Let me in! Are you all right?" It was Mama. Desperation filled her voice.

"Just a minute!" I climbed out of the tub, dried off quickly, jumped into my clothes, and opened the door.

"Oh, my God! You could have been killed!" Mama hugged me. The noise outside was deafening. Sirens were shrilling, people were screaming.

"We must go down to the bomb shelter immediately," Mama urged.

Each of us carried a mattress and a pillow down the staircase to the basement. The neighbors were heading in the same direction. The noise outside was growing even louder.

Downstairs, we were able to find enough room to stay together on the cement floor. At least two hundred people were packed like matches in a box in the cold basement. The noise outside didn't cease for days. Every now and then, a few brave souls made their way upstairs to the various kitchens and collected whatever meager supplies were left. Several women made thin soup and boiled potatoes on the janitor's ancient stove. But most of the time, we went hungry. In spite of the din outside, however, the crowd was surprisingly full of laughter and high hopes. All of us realized that the heavy mortar attack meant that the Soviet troops couldn't be far behind, and that they were getting the upper hand. A rumor that the Soviets had surrounded Budapest cheered our hearts. They were calling through megaphones, ordering the Arrow Cross and the Germans to lay down their arms. We greeted the arrival of the New Year with fervent prayers for the war to be over.

"This can't last much longer," Ervin said one morning. "I'm going outside to look around."

"I'll come with you," Gabor volunteered.

"Absolutely not!" Mama was vehement. "I couldn't bear it if anything happened to either one of you after all we've suffered. It would kill me. You'll wait here."

One look at her determined face convinced the boys to co-operate. For the next two weeks, Ervin and Gabor, like the rest of us, whiled away their time in complete boredom and ever-increasing hope. Early on the morning of January 16, my brother shook me awake. The others were still asleep. I could see the excitement on Ervin's thin face.

"Listen!" he said. "Just listen!"

I did as I was told. For a minute, I was completely puzzled. I heard nothing, not a sound.

"What are you talking about?"

"Listen!" he insisted.

Suddenly, I realized what he meant. It was so quiet outside that you could have heard a bird chirping. Ervin and I stared at each other, then I jumped out of bed, put on my shoes, and threw Mama's coat over my clothes. We tumbled up the staircase leading to the front entrance of the building, pushed open the heavy door to the courtyard, and peeked out. A soldier in a dark green uniform and a fur hat with a five-pointed red star on it was opening the iron gate of the front garden. He saw us at the same time as we saw him. He said something in a language we couldn't understand and pointed his rifle at us.

"The Soviets are here! The war must be over!" Ervin crowed with joy.

He grabbed my hands and we jumped up and down, whooping with happiness. The soldier seemed puzzled. He kept his rifle pointed at us.

"We're your friends! Welcome!" I told him.

We tried approaching him, but he backed away with a bewildered expression. He didn't seem to understand me. Nor did he lower his rifle. I pointed to the canary yellow star sewn onto Mama's coat. I tore the star off, threw it on the ground, and trampled it into the dirty snow with the heel of my shoe. Comprehension dawned on the soldier's face and he lowered his gun.

We ran up to him. Ervin shook his hand, and I kissed him on the cheek.

Epilogue

Two days later, we moved back to Aunt Miriam's apartment. The couple who had been living there abandoned it and returned to their country home. Although we were happy to be back, the familiar rooms echoed with the laughter and tears of our beloved dead. Mama and Mrs. Grof stood guard by the front windows – waiting and waiting for any of our missing relatives to turn up.

While they maintained their vigil, Ervin, Gabor, and I went to the offices of the International Red Cross, where we found out about the unspeakable horrors of the concentration camps and the martyrdom of millions of Jewish men, women, and children. We scanned the lists of camp survivors, but none of the names we hoped to find ever appeared.

Mama and Mrs. Grof did not give up. They never left their post by the windows – day after day, week after week, month after month. But no one they were waiting for ever turned the corner of our street. After a long, long time, even these two desperate women stopped waiting.

Life went on. We even learned how to be happy again, but nothing was ever the same as before.

Historical Note

To save one life is as if you have saved the world.
                                        – The Talmud

There really was a Swedish diplomat called Raoul Wallenberg, and he was a true hero. Wallenberg saved the world over and over again, rescuing 100,000 Jewish men, women, and children during the six months that he spent in Budapest, Hungary, during the Holocaust. Many of the Hungarian Jews who owed their lives to Wallenberg's courage and goodness were young people like Marta, Ervin, and Gabor in *My Canary Yellow Star*.

By the time Wallenberg arrived in Budapest in July 1944, the Hungarian countryside had been emptied of its Jewish inhabitants. More than 430,000 Jews had already been deported to concentration camps like Auschwitz in

Poland, most of them never to return. However, another 230,000 Jews still remained in Budapest. Wallenberg saved the lives of thousands of these people by issuing them Schutz-Passes, Swedish protective passports. He also sheltered more than 20,000 Jews in the International Ghetto in Swedish-protected safe houses and saved the lives of many more by pulling them off the trains that were waiting to transport them to death camps in Poland and Germany. Through skilled diplomacy, Wallenberg prevented the Germans and the Arrow Cross from massacring the 70,000 Jewish inhabitants of the large Budapest Ghetto at the end of the war, and from dynamiting the Ghetto itself.

On January 17, 1944, the day Pest was liberated by the Soviets, Wallenberg, his driver, and a Soviet guard left for the town of Debrecen, where the Soviet headquarters were located. Wallenberg wanted to present his plans for relief work in war-ravaged Hungary and for the restoration of stolen Jewish property. He never returned from this trip. He seemed to have vanished from the face of the earth.

For many, many years, people believed that Wallenberg was still alive in the terrible prisons of the former Soviet Union. Others insisted that he was shot at the infamous Lubyanka prison soon after the end of the war. None of the rumors was ever substantiated. In late 2000, the Russians did admit that they had suspected Wallenberg of being an American spy and had wrongfully imprisoned him. But they stopped short of fully explaining what had happened

Raoul Wallenberg

to him. In January 2001, a joint Russian-Swedish commit-tee released a report that reached no definitive conclusion about Wallenberg's fate. The Russians returned to a long-held claim that he had died of a heart attack in prison in 1947. He would have been thirty-five. The Swedish offi-cials, on the other hand, maintained that it is still unclear if Wallenberg is dead or alive. Only one thing is certain: Raoul Wallenberg, a beacon of decency in a most indecent world, was never heard from again.

GLOSSARY

bar mitzvah	a religious ceremony for Jewish boys when they reach thirteen
cantor	a person who chants and leads the prayers in a synagogue
chala	a bread made with eggs, traditionally eaten on Shabbos
cholent	a traditional Jewish Shabbos dish usually made with meat and vegetables and allowed to cook overnight
menorah	a candelabrum with eight branches used during Hanukah
nokedli	Hungarian dumplings
Rosh Hashanah	the Jewish New Year
Shabbos	the Jewish Sabbath, or day of rest and religious observance
Shema	a Jewish declaration of faith used as an important prayer
tallis (pl. tallisim)	a prayer shawl
Torah	the first five books of the Bible; also called the Pentateuch
yarmulke	a skullcap worn by Jewish men
Yom Kippur	a sacred Jewish holy day marked by fasting and prayers of repentance; falls eight days after Rosh Hashanah